*To Marty,
with best wishes
Carol Roth*

FORGET ME NOT

FORGET ME NOT

Carol Roth

Clouse Publishing, Library, Pennsylvania

Copyright © 1998 by Carol Roth

All Rights Reserved

Clouse Publishing
P. O. Box 32
Library, PA 15129

The names, characters, places and events in this book are fictitious and any resemblance to actual persons, living or dead, is purely coincidental.

ISBN 0-9667555-4-5

Cover by Kelly Mayhew

Printed in the United States of America

In Memory of my grandmother,

Emma Carroll

FORGET ME NOT

~ ONE ~

Emilia studied the pin lying on her desk. She turned it over. The inscription read,
"Down by the seashore carved on a rock, three little words – forget me not." The pin was unique, hand carved by someone with exquisite taste and a talent to match. Her mother wore this unusual pin for as long as Emilia could remember. The inscription blurred as tears welled up in her eyes from a pang of sorrow as she thought of her mother.

She vaguely remembered that her mother received the pin from a dear friend many years ago, but to her recollection the mysterious friend was never identified. Emilia wondered now whether this was an oversight or by design.

She discovered the pin was missing shortly after her mother's death. When all efforts to find it failed, she cried until her eyes were red and swollen and her head throbbed. The monetary value meant nothing to her. She wanted it for a keepsake because it represented something or someone very special to her mother.

Then yesterday, two months later and completely out of the blue, it reappeared by way of introduction from a Mr. Dennis McClelland. The note, which accompanied the pin, gave no explanation, merely asked to see her as soon as possible on a personal matter.

Emilia wondered how the pin came to be in the possession of this Mr. McClelland, but he had returned it and she was grateful. Although she didn't think it was a good idea, she agreed to see him today at two o'clock in her office.

A knock at her door reminded her it was two o'clock. Dennis McClelland was right on time.

"Miss Wright, I'm very happy to meet you," he said, as Emilia's secretary, Irene, showed him in.

Emilia shook his hand and noticed how striking he was. He was dressed conservatively and seemed sure of himself. He looked to be about 45 years old, six feet or so, black hair, dark brown eyes and in great physical shape.

"I'm very glad to meet you," she responded. She offered him a chair. "Please sit down."

Dennis sat down in the chair opposite her desk and placed his briefcase by his side. Emilia noticed his look of approval and thought she detected a definite twinkle in his eye when he looked at her. She suspected he had a wonderful sense of humor.

"I'd like to thank you for returning the pin. It means a great deal to me."

"You're quite welcome," he said with a broad smile.

Emilia's breath caught at the appearance of deep dimples in his cheeks. His smile is enough to melt a block of ice she thought. She was relaxed and completely at ease in his company.

"Have we met before?" she asked.

"No, I don't think so," he replied. "I'm sure I'd remember if we had."

Emilia again sensed that look of approval.

"Tell me, where did you find the pin and how did you know it belonged to me?" she asked.

"Actually, I didn't find it," he said. "I'm a private investigator and I returned it on behalf of a client who wanted to be sure you received the pin, as well as his personal invitation."

"Invitation to what?" she asked. "And just who is your client?"

"His name is Brad Owensford," he answered.

Emilia stiffened and her sense of ease was immediately replaced by obvious annoyance. Her eyes, warm and friendly just moments before, were now turned on Dennis McClelland with unconcealed dislike. Emilia knew he was aware of the impact the name of Brad Owensford had on her. She was not very good at hiding her feelings, especially negative ones.

The name, as well as the reputation, was familiar to Emilia. In her opinion, it was synonymous with the power responsible for the corruption and demoralization of the country over the past few decades. Mr. Owensford was the largest financial supporter of the American Personal Liberties Association.

Emilia was sorry she had ever agreed to see Dennis McClelland and wanted to end this meeting as quickly as possible.

"Mr. McClelland, would you please get to the point." She knew she was on the brink of rudeness but really didn't care. She just wanted to get him out of her office.

"Yes, of course," he said. "I'm sorry if I've upset you."

"I'm sure you realized that was a possibility if you're aware of your client's reputation, and I feel certain you are. Now please get on with it so we can conclude this meeting," she said in an icy tone.

"Brad Owensford has instructed me to extend his invitation to an informal dinner party he is giving at his home in East Sandwich on the Cape next Friday evening. At that time, he wishes to personally speak to you with regard to the pin. He particularly wanted me to stress that it is of the utmost importance and in your own best interest that you accept his invitation."

Emilia thought she was hearing things. What he said made no sense at all. Why would a perfect stranger invite her to a dinner party? And the way the so-called invitation had been presented was actually bizarre. In fact, the innuendo was as close to a threat as she ever heard. Perhaps she was becoming paranoid. She decided she had to respond in no uncertain terms.

"Mr. McClelland, I have no intention of accepting such an invitation. I'm afraid it would be quite impossible." She stood up.

"Now, if you'll excuse me, I must get ready for my next appointment." Emilia hit the intercom and snapped, "Irene, please come in and bring your notebook. Mr. McClelland is just leaving." She knew Irene, who worked for her for the last eight years, would respond at once when she heard the tone of her voice.

Emilia knew her behavior was extremely rude and unprofessional. She actually resented Dennis McClelland for placing her in this awkward position. She watched as he stood up, grabbed his briefcase and headed for the door without so much as a word. She assumed that being a gentleman is all that kept him from reacting in turn. She hated to admit it, but she admired him for that quality.

Irene was on her way in just as Dennis opened the door to leave. Emilia heard Irene thank him for holding the door and he responded by telling Irene to have a nice afternoon. He mumbled that one of them should.

When Irene came in, Emilia motioned for her to sit down.

"I'm sorry I snapped at you," she said. "I've had better days."

"Did you find out how he got the pin?" Irene asked as she dropped into the chair just vacated by Dennis.

"Yes, I found out how Dennis McClelland got the pin. He was returning it on behalf of a client. Guess who the client was? None other than Brad Owensford. Now you can understand why I was so upset."

"Don't you have any idea how Brad Owensford got it?" Irene asked.

"No, I don't. If I have to see him personally to find out, I'd rather never know."

Emilia told Irene about the invitation and it sounded even more unbelievable than it did the first time around. Emilia was certain she had done the right thing. The whole incident was best forgotten. Or so she thought.

Emilia spent the balance of the afternoon working on a new brochure and it was close to 5:30 when she and Irene left the office. It had been an exceptionally busy day. Emilia was the manager of the Plymouth Chapter of 'Smokers Cessation, Inc.' and had been for the past fifteen years. Her staff consisted of ten seminar moderators, two clerks and one secretary, as opposed to two moderators and one secretary when she began. The largest segment of their business was with the corporations who were obligated by law to provide a smoke-free environment for their employees.

When the Surgeon General's report on the hazards of smoking was first published, it had little effect on the majority of hard-core smokers. Even a later release on the hazards of second-hand smoke did little to change the overall statistics. But when the story of the conspiracy to addict the public by deliberately increasing the amount of nicotine in tobacco products hit the stands, there was a virtual stampede.

Emilia liked her job. She liked to help people regain control of their lives. She taught about the potential quality of life and demonstrated the insidious way any addiction is detrimental to its fulfillment. Her dedication earned her the highest success rate in the Eastern Regional Office.

Emilia locked the door and asked Irene to join her for dinner. "We'll try that new restaurant that opened on the waterfront last week. I think it's called Sam's Seafood."

"Sounds good to me," Irene was quick to respond. I don't have to be home until eight o'clock.

They got in the car and as Emilia headed toward the waterfront, she noticed the traffic was exceptionally light for a Monday night. Better enjoy it while it lasts, she thought. The tourist season would officially get underway in about two weeks. Most of the onslaught was felt on the Cape itself, but Plymouth got its share, particularly Plymouth Plantation, which was only a few miles from town. As they discussed the events of the day, Emilia knew that Irene was about to tease her about Dennis McClelland when she heard that silly giggle.

"You know, Emilia, you may have been a little hasty today," Irene said. "That Dennis McClelland was awfully good looking. It's not his fault he just happens to work for a noxious employer. Doesn't mean he sanctions what Brad Owensford stands for. I mean, everybody has to work."

Emilia laughed. "Perhaps I did overreact," she said. "I bet Dennis McClelland is already on his way back to the Cape."

As they pulled into the parking lot at the restaurant, Emilia noticed that the same car, which was behind them when they left the office, pulled in also. Could that just be a coincidence she wondered? It seemed her imagination was running rampant ever since Dennis McClelland's visit.

The waitress showed them to a very nice table overlooking the water. They both ordered 'Spots,' the catch of the day. The client who recommended the restaurant did not exaggerate one bit. The food was excellent.

"Oh, look, there's Chuck Collins," Emilia said. "I haven't seen him for ages. It looks like he's alone. I wonder if he'd like to join us?" She waved when Chuck looked their way.

Chuck Collins, the Superintendent of the Plymouth School District, was very instrumental in obtaining a government grant that paid for smoking cessation seminars in the schools. Emilia, Chuck and Irene had become good friends while working together on the project.

"He saw us," Emilia said. "He's coming over."

"Well, you never know who you're going to run into," Chuck said "I'm glad to see you both looking so well. It's been a long time. How is everything?"

"Just fine," Emilia replied. "Would you like to join us? We just started eating and we're going to have coffee afterward."

"I'd love to but I'm afraid I'll have to take a rain check," Chuck replied. "I'm dining with two of my teachers who requested an impromptu meeting. It's about some kind of confrontation with the American Personal Liberties Association and has all the earmarks of a serious situation."

"This is the second time today I've heard that name," Emilia said. "What do they have to do with the schools?"

"Not too much yet, but that organization is getting to be a thorn in my side," Chuck said. "Every time I turn around there seems to be something going on to undermine the Public School System. They are currently questioning our control over the curriculum that's being taught to the children. In fact, they wish to introduce some subject matter that is questionable to say the very least."

"I'm sure the parents will have something to say about that," Emilia said.

"That's what bothers me most," Chuck said. "The lethargy on the part of the parents."

"That's too bad," Emilia said. "I wish you luck. If it's any consolation, you're not the only one they're picking on."

"I'll keep that in mind," Chuck said. "Well, take care and I'll see you ladies later."

Emilia watched as Chuck followed the waitress to his table.

"Chuck is such a nice person," Irene said. "I can remember when he first took over as Superintendent of Schools. He's doing an outstanding job."

Emilia couldn't agree more. Sipping her coffee, she said, "I sure do sympathize with the frustration he must be feeling. They say you can't fight city hall and they're right about that. On the other hand, I can understand that, in all good conscience, he's got to try."

In Emilia's judgment, the American Personal Liberties Association was responsible for pulling off the largest fraud ever perpetrated against this country, that our constitution advocated the separation of church and state. She wondered if the American people had forgotten that ours was a Christian nation founded under God, and freedom of religion was guaranteed to everyone. Now, it appears we have freedom from religion rather than freedom of religion she thought.

"Irene," Emilia asked, "Do you ever think about the way our nation has seemed to turn its back on God? I sometimes wonder how much depravation God will tolerate before we are punished."

"I try not to think about it," Irene replied. "I know we're in a pretty bad state of affairs, and nobody is doing anything about it. I think the American people better wake up and smell the roses. It's a pretty scary scenario."

When they left the restaurant, Emilia dropped Irene off, stopped at the deli for cold cuts and milk, and then started home. She looked in her rear view mirror to change lanes and saw the car that pulled in after her at the restaurant behind her again. She was sure of it. It couldn't be a coincidence this time. There must be some logical explanation she thought. There wouldn't be any reason for anyone to follow her. None the less, she was glad her apartment was in a secured building with its own parking facilities.

Emilia parked in her assigned space, took the elevator up to the second floor and entered her apartment. She locked the door and, without turning on the light, walked across the room and looked out the window. The car was parked across the street. As she strained to see who was in it, the car pulled away. It was probably someone dropping off another tenant she thought. But the uneasy feeling lingered.

- *TWO* -

When Dennis got back to the Seaside Inn, where he registered that morning, he went directly to his room, changed his clothes and headed out for a brisk walk before dinner. He definitely needed to unwind after his meeting with Emilia Wright.

The muscles in his neck actually ached from tightening up when she became angry and practically threw him out of her office. He never expected their meeting to end on such a sour note, especially since they seemed to be so compatible at first.

He began to jog as he recalled the meeting. He hated to admit it, but she was right. He should have expected her negative reaction when he mentioned Brad's name.

He was aware of Brad's reputation, due to his association with the American Personal Liberties Association, and he had grown accustomed to the negative response it generated. But there was another side to Brad that most people never knew. He was a philanthropist and supported many charitable organizations in his community.

Dennis worked on several cases for Brad over the last thirteen years, but he had little knowledge of his personal life. He was a bachelor by choice. Parents dead many years. One brother living in Chicago. One niece living on the Cape. This was the extent of what Dennis knew. He also knew that he had developed a genuine fondness and respect for Brad Owensford over the years.

Dennis ran about five miles before he did his stretching routine and headed back to the Inn. The exercise eased the tense knotted muscles but he still needed a little work on his ego.

After a shower and a change of clothes, he headed to the dining room for dinner. Although he didn't feel hungry, he ordered the sirloin steak special. It turned out to be delicious, and he savored every bite. It suddenly dawned on him that he forgot to eat lunch.

He returned to his room around seven o'clock. It was so stuffy, he opened the balcony doors and went to sit outside and look at the ocean while his room cooled off. The night was exceptionally warm and he relished the feel of the light breeze on his face.

His thoughts drifted to Emilia Wright. He'd taken care of Brad's business, but in the process lost any hope he had of seeing her again. Why did it matter so much? Common sense told him he had just met her. What did he really know about her? Yet there was something so appealing. She was indeed attractive; strawberry blond hair worn short and naturally curly, large bluish-gray eyes, fine delicate features and, of course, that splash of freckles running across her nose and cheeks. But, aside from the superficial, there shone a wholesomeness, uncommonly rare in today's world.

The ringing of the phone cut short his reverie. Annoyed by the interruption, but aware it must be Brad, he hurried inside and answered.

"Denny, how did it go?" Brad asked. "Did she say she'd come?"

He tried to block out the eagerness in Brad's voice. He replied, "No, she indicated she has no intention of accepting your invitation, that it would be quite impossible." Dennis tried to soften Brad's disappointment and added, "She was sincerely glad to get the pin."

"Denny, I've got to see her," he said. "I don't care how you do it but I must see her before it's too late." Brad was up in years but Dennis was certain that wasn't what he meant by "before it's too late".

"Brad, I'm not trying to pry," Dennis said as he kicked off his shoes and sat down on a chair. "But perhaps if you'd fill me in on the specifics of the situation, I'd have more luck getting her to see you." There was a long pause and Dennis knew Brad was considering whether to confide in him. He sensed that Brad was under a tremendous amount of stress and it somehow emanated from the unresolved solution concerning Emilia. As he waited for Brad to answer, Dennis walked over and shut the balcony doors.

"All right," Brad said. "In order to fill you in on everything, I'd have to go back almost forty-five years and we don't have the luxury of time on our side right now." With anguish in his voice, he blurted out, "Emilia is my daughter and she is in grave danger."

"She's your daughter!" Dennis exclaimed. He was sure Emilia didn't know. Her reaction to Brad's name was the only confirmation he needed for that deduction.

"I'm sorry," Dennis said. "Please go on. Tell me the rest of it." As he waited for Brad to continue, Dennis reached over to the table and poured himself a drink of water.

"You can't divulge what I've disclosed to you," Brad said. "She wouldn't accept it in a million years. I didn't know myself until several years later. The man she believed, all her life, to be her father died two years ago. His name was Robert Wright. He and Katherine were married seven months before Emilia was born."

Dennis interrupted. "Does anyone else know about this?" He put the phone in his other hand while he looked for a pencil and paper to make notes.

"Denny, that's why I'm worried sick. It all started back then . . .the mysterious disappearance of Emilia's uncle, the untimely death of her grandmother and the blackmail which continues to this day."

Dennis rubbed his forehead. He was absolutely astounded. "Brad, you know we're going to have to resolve this entire matter as soon as possible. In the meantime, what can we do to ensure Emilia's safety?" He sensed there were dirty politics involved and was sure the little he'd heard so far would turn out to be just the tip of the iceberg. His heart skipped a beat and his legs got weak when he thought of Emilia being in danger.

Dennis noticed as Brad continued that he sounded weary but relieved after sharing his burden. He could certainly understand that.

Brad said, "Tell her I was engaged to her mother, many years ago before she married. That when she became ill, she sent me a pin I'd given her when we broke up and I just had a feeling she wanted me to meet her daughter. That was why she sent me the pin."

"Did Katherine ever find out you knew Emilia was your daughter?" Dennis asked when Brad paused.

"That's something I guess I'll never know," Brad replied. "I only know there is someone out there who does know. Someone so consumed with hate he never hesitated to use that knowledge to force my financial assistance in support of the APLA." Dennis realized Brad was an unwilling pawn in this organization. He should have known Brad would never support such an anti-American group by choice.

Dennis tried to alleviate Brad's concern. He said, "I'll give her a call tonight and tell her what you suggested and see if that does the trick. If I can't get in touch with her tonight, I'll try first thing in the morning." He opened the drawer of the table to see if there was a phone book.

"Please do whatever you can," Brad said.

"I will," Dennis promised. "I may have to tell her more than you want, but it might become necessary. It's not fair to expose her to possible danger without at least alerting her to its existence. I'll get back to you as soon as I've seen her."

"Thanks Denny," Brad said. "I don't know what I'd do without you."

Dennis hung up the phone. He had no idea how he was going to convince Emilia to trust him. He decided to use honesty. It was the best approach he knew, but he would only reveal as much as Brad wanted her to know, if at all possible.

While he looked for her number in the phone book, he rehearsed what he would say when she answered. As he dialed the phone, he found himself grateful for any motive, which allowed him the opportunity of seeing her again.

He frowned in disappointment when he got her answering machine. He looked at his watch and saw that it was only eight o'clock. She probably stopped for dinner on the way home from the office. When the beep sounded to leave a message, he said, "Miss Wright, this is Dennis McClelland. Would you please call me when you get in, no matter what time? Did you know that Brad Owensford was once engaged to you mother? He desperately wants to see you. Please call me. I'm staying at the Seaside Inn, Room 614."

- *THREE* -

As Emilia walked away from the window, she noticed the flashing light on her answering machine. She felt weak in the knees after she played the message from Dennis McClelland. It left her no choice. She would have to return his call. There were far too many unanswered questions in her past. She knew if she didn't return his call, she would always wonder about the relationship between Brad Owensford and her mother. Emilia really wanted to know how Brad Owensford got her mother's pin.

She made a cup of tea and then looked up the number of the Seaside Inn. Her hand was shaking as she dialed the number. She asked for Room 614 and waited impatiently while they put her call through.

"Hello," Dennis answered quickly.

He must have been sitting on the phone, Emilia thought. "Hello, Mr. McClelland, this is Emilia Wright. I just got home a few minutes ago and got your message. I'm returning your call as I'm sure you knew I would."

"I've been pacing the floor waiting for you to call," he said. "I really have to talk to you."

"I think that might be a good idea, Mr. McClelland," she replied. "I would like to know a little more about Brad Owensford and my mother being engaged."

"Please, could we dispense with the formality? My friends call me Denny and I do want to be your friend."

"All right Denny, if you'll call me Emilia."

"Look," he said, "It's only nine o'clock. Would you mind if I come over there? I'd much rather discuss this in person. I promise I'll only stay an hour. Believe me, I'm not being trite when I say it could be a matter of life and death."

So, the cloak and dagger scenario she thought to be the result of an overactive imagination was not a far-fetched notion. She shivered with a sense of apprehension as she gave him directions to her apartment. After she hung up, she had second thoughts about letting him come over. But it was too late now; he was on his way.

Emilia went down to the lobby when the security guard rang up to tell her Dennis had arrived. He had already signed in and was waiting by the elevator when the door opened.

"You sure made good time," she said as he got on the elevator.

"I left as soon as I hung up the phone," he replied. "The traffic was light. I don't think I stopped for a single red light."

They went into the living room and she offered him a seat. "Can I get you something to drink? I'm going to have a cup of tea."

"No, thanks, I don't care for anything right now," he replied as he sat down on the sofa. "I'm glad you agreed to see me," she heard him call after her as she headed for the kitchen.

Emilia came back minutes later with her tea and sat down in the chair opposite the sofa. She got a coaster and put the cup of hot tea down on the table beside her.

"You know I'm here to persuade you to see Brad Owensford, " Dennis said. "I know you've already refused, but I'm hoping that what you've learned about your mother and Brad will change your mind."

"I know Brad told you that he and my mother were once engaged. I don't know this to be a fact, and neither do you. Since he had the pin, I suppose we've got to believe she did send it to him. There doesn't seem to be any other plausible explanation. Why do you think she sent it to him?"

Emilia asked. She carefully took a sip of her tea while she waited to hear if he had any idea.

"I really don't know," Dennis answered.

She sensed he was a little more relaxed than he had been in her office as he leaned back against the pillows. She was sorry she had been so rude earlier. Emilia hoped he realized her reaction to Brad Owensford's name was not characteristic of her usual temperament.

"Think back," Dennis said. "Did you ever hear anything about your mother being engaged to someone else before she met your father?"

"I've been thinking about that since you called," she replied.

"Have you come up with anything," he asked.

"I vaguely remember my Aunt Elizabeth talking about someone my mother was crazy about and would have married in a heartbeat. The only problem was his family. They were very wealthy, which was one stumbling block they could have overcome. They were also Catholic and they were adamant that their son should marry someone of his own faith."

"That is absolutely ludicrous," he said in astonishment. "Why didn't they run away and get married?"

"I don't know," Emilia said and put down her cup. "Perhaps that isn't an option in some social circles. My aunt said he begged my mother to turn Catholic. She, being a staunch Lutheran, refused. That's about the extent of what I can remember."

"Brad is Catholic," Dennis said. "I know that for a fact. He is very wealthy. His father was a well known philanthropist and left his entire fortune to Brad." Emilia noticed how he ran his hand through his hair as he tried to rationalize what she had just said.

"Strange, how differently people, raised under identical circumstances, will react when faced with the same situation," Emilia mused. "My Aunt Elizabeth, who was also a staunch Lutheran, agreed to turn Catholic when she married my uncle. There were some family members who say she was bribed with a fur coat. True or not, I don't know."

Dennis laughed. "Does what you remember mean you'll go with me tomorrow? I sure hope so."

Emilia stood up and walked over to look out the window. "I don't know. I really don't think I should. It won't change anything," she said. "What possible reason would he have for wanting to meet me? What happened between them was a long time ago. It had nothing to do with me then and it surely doesn't have anything to do with me now. It won't change my opinion of him and the way I feel about the organization he endorses today. I'm sure he can't be the same man my mother loved. She had better taste than that."

She closed the drapes and returned to her chair.

"Did your mother only have one sister?" he asked. Emilia was glad he changed the subject.

"Yes," she said. "She also had two brothers. My Uncle Jim died when I was only five. I never knew my Uncle Andrew. He disappeared before I was born. He went to the store to buy a loaf of bread and was never seen again. Hard to believe, isn't it? But then they say truth is stranger than fiction."

"Yes, it is," he said. "Do you recall any speculation about what could have happened to him?"

"I heard that my grandmother hired a private detective, who traced him as far as Chicago. The trail ended there."

"She never heard from him again?" Dennis asked.

"No," Emilia said. "According to my mother, she died in her sleep a few weeks later. She wasn't sick, but she'd had a chronic heart condition all her life. The death certificate showed the cause of death to be a coronary infarction. My mother was the one who found her."

"Is your father still living?" he asked.

"No," Emilia replied. "He died about two years ago."

"Getting back to Brad," she said. "That invitation you delivered sounded more like a threat than an invitation."

"He didn't mean it that way at all," Dennis said. "It's just that he's concerned for your safety."

"Do you realize I've been uneasy ever since you left my office this afternoon? Just what is this matter of life and death you referred to when you called?" She heard the anxiety in her own voice as she continued.

"I've even imagined there was a car that followed me when Irene and I left the office to go to dinner. Then, I was sure that same car followed me home. I almost reported it before I convinced myself it was just a coincidence."

Dennis got up and began to pace. "Believe me, I don't know what it's all about," he said. "I know Brad thinks you're in danger. After what you've just told me, I'm inclined to agree. If it makes any difference, I'd hate like the devil to see anything happen to you."

"Thanks," she said. "I know you're just trying to help and I do appreciate it."

"Then you will go?" he asked. "Please say yes and put my mind at ease."

"OK," Emilia said. "On one condition."

"What's the condition," he asked. He walked over, sat down again on the sofa and waited for her answer.

"If you'll promise not to leave me when we get there," she said. "I don't want to be left alone with Brad Owensford."

"It's a deal," he replied. "Will you be able to leave first thing in the morning? The sooner we go, the better it will be."

"I suppose so," she said. "I'll call Irene and let her know I won't be in tomorrow morning so she doesn't schedule any appointments."

"Maybe you better tell her not to schedule anything until she hears from you," he said. "Brad might want us to stay overnight."

Emilia glared at Dennis with a disgusted look. "I certainly hope not," she said. "I'm afraid I'd have a little problem with that."

"I think you might be pleasantly surprised when you meet Brad. You may even like him. He's very personable."

"I can assure you I will not like him," Emilia said. "He may be very charming, but what he stands for is not. I couldn't possibly like anyone who financially supports the APLA. You must be aware of the damage that organization has done to our country. You'd have to be blind not to see it."

"He may have no choice," Dennis said. "Let's give him the benefit of the doubt. You could be wrong about him. There could be extenuating circumstances that make it impossible for him to refuse to help them."

"How can you say he has no choice?" Emilia asked and gave him an angry look. "I think we all have a choice about what we support." She felt that Dennis was more than a little annoyed with her.

"Wait until you meet him," he said. "I know you'll change your mind about him. I guarantee it."

"Well, there's no use arguing about it," she said. "We just don't see eye to eye on this and probably never will."

"Hey, remember me?" he asked. "I'm the one who wants to be your friend."

Emilia suddenly laughed. "I'm sorry," she said. "The APLA is something I feel very strongly about. I would make a wonderful activist, don't you think?"

"I sure wouldn't want you demonstrating at my meeting," Dennis said. He stretched and looked at his watch. "Hey, it's 10:30 and I promised I'd only stay an hour. What time shall I pick you up in the morning? How does seven o'clock sound? We'll get an early start and beat the traffic. We can stop for breakfast on the way."

"That's fine." Emilia walked him to the door. When her hand accidentally touched his, her heart began to beat faster. She felt weak and flushed from a powerful physical attraction. She wondered if he felt it too.

- *FOUR* -

Dennis got back to the Inn about 10:45 and immediately dialed Brad's number. Even though it was a little late, he knew his call would be welcome. Brad would be relieved to hear that Emilia had agreed to see him.

Dennis heard the apprehension in Brad's voice when he answered the phone.

"Brad, it's Dennis. I've got good news and knew you'd want to hear right away. Emilia and I will be arriving sometime tomorrow morning."

"Thank God," Brad said. "How much did you have to tell her?"

"Not too much," Dennis replied. "Just that you and Katherine were once engaged. I told her you felt certain she was in some kind of danger. Of course, she questioned that. I persuaded her that the only way to get to the bottom of it would be to talk to you." Dennis took off his shoes and collapsed in a chair. He suddenly felt tired. He'd had a long day.

"And how did she feel about that?" Brad asked. "Since she emphatically refused the first invitation, I suppose I already know the answer to that one. I'd prefer to believe she was coming because she was anxious to meet me, but I know that wouldn't be realistic. The important thing is, she's coming. For right now, that's enough." Dennis could hear Brad getting ice and pouring a drink.

"Brad," Dennis asked, "I know it's none of my business, but is it true that you and Katherine never got married because she refused to turn Catholic? That's what Emilia remembers her aunt telling her." Dennis heard Brad choke on his drink at the unexpected question. "Are you all right?" he asked.

"Yes," Brad replied in a hoarse voice. "You just took me by surprise. There is an element of truth in it, but it's a far cry from the whole story."

Dennis sensed that Brad was reluctant to discuss it. "Maybe we can talk about it some other time," he said. Dennis got up out of the chair, picked up the phone and walked over to sit on the bed.

"It certainly is irrelevant to the matter at hand," Brad said. "Our prime objective is to convince Emilia that she is in danger. If at all possible, I'd like to accomplish that without revealing our relationship. It won't be easy, given the fact that her safety is the price offered, in exchange for my continued support of the APLA."

Dennis stretched out on the bed and waited for Brad to continue.

"Actually, the threat included both Katherine and Emilia," he said. "Now that Katherine is gone, Emilia is the only hold they have on me. I believe they are unscrupulous enough to do whatever it takes to keep me in line. That's why I'm so concerned for her."

Dennis felt his arm going to sleep. He put the phone in his other hand and turned over on the bed. "Do you have any idea who's behind it?" he asked. "I mean, extortion is a serious criminal offense. The ultimate objective would have to be of paramount importance to risk imprisonment if caught and convicted. From what you've told me, the informant would have to be someone with access to first hand knowledge about you and Katherine. How many people know that Emilia is your child? It's got to be someone who was, or is, close to you. In all likelihood, it's someone you'd never suspect."

"I have no idea," Brad said. "I do know that the money ultimately ends up in the hands of the APLA, where I am listed as their largest financial supporter. It's like living a lie most of your life."

Dennis tried to imagine himself in Brad's position, with the frustration Brad must have endured over the years, and wondered how he would deal with this current situation. He could appreciate why Brad was concerned for Emilia. His own apprehension was growing by the minute.

"Brad," he said, "I think I understand how you feel. Try to get a good night's sleep. When we get there tomorrow, you'll just have to play it by ear. As you said, our main objective will be to convince her she's in danger. If it becomes necessary to tell her everything, then so be it. Maybe it's better to get it out in the open. It won't expose her to any more danger than she is already in."

Dennis again urged Brad to get a good night's sleep and said he would see him sometime in the morning.

After he hung up, he immediately got undressed, turned out the light and got into bed. As an afterthought, he called the desk and left an order for a wake up call.

Dennis awoke to the ringing of the telephone. He groaned and turned over. For one brief moment, he forgot he was at the Seaside Inn and had requested a wake up call for 6:00 a.m. It was just a precaution since he was usually wide-awake by 5:30. His foresight about the need for a wake up call could be the beginning of a well-organized day, he thought, as he went into the bathroom to take a shower.

He got dressed and went down to the lobby. There were no messages and he checked out. The accommodations had been excellent and he made a mental note to stop here, if his travels took him to the area again.

He smiled at the thought of seeing Emilia. Better curb any rambunctious behavior. He sure didn't want to scare her off. Did people actually fall in love at first sight? Or was it simply infatuation? Or worse yet, lust? He didn't think so. There was no doubt he was attracted to her physically. When their hands accidentally touched while walking to her door last night, it was all he could do to keep his hands off her. He actually fought an urge to take her in his arms. I must be slipping he thought.

Then he realized there was something more . . . a tender, passionate desire to protect and care for her. In addition, he genuinely liked her. He had dated in the past, but his anticipation at seeing her again reminded him of a schoolboy with a crush on his first grade teacher.

During the ten-minute drive to her place, he found himself hoping their short trip would prove to be uneventful. There was a certain hazardous atmosphere surrounding this whole business with Brad. Forget it, he told himself, you're just being an alarmist looking for calamities where none exist. In the broad light of day, he wondered if Brad had blown the whole thing out of proportion. Dennis preferred that scenario because of his concern for Emilia.

- FIVE -

Emilia was sitting outside waiting for him. "You're right on time," she said as he opened the door for her. "Isn't this a beautiful day?"

"There couldn't be a better day to go for a ride," Dennis agreed. "I know a marvelous restaurant about five miles before we get to the Canal. It's right before you go over the bridge to the Cape. We'll stop there and have breakfast if that's OK with you."

"Anywhere is fine," Emilia said. "I'll just relax and enjoy the scenery."

She's even more beautiful early in the morning he thought. Although dressed in casual attire, she was still a knockout. She was wearing a plain dark green silk pants suit, a long gold chain with several charms, and gold hoop earrings. Simple yet sophisticated. She was a very classy lady. And he knew by the hollow feeling in the pit of his stomach that he was falling . . . hook, line and sinker.

"I called Irene last night and told her I wouldn't be in," Emilia said. "Told her I'd get back to her sometime today. Did you call Brad Owensford and tell him we were coming?"

"I sure did," Dennis replied. "He's really looking forward to meeting you."

"I wish I could say the same," Emilia sighed. "You know I'm only going because I have no other choice."

"I understand that," Dennis said. "If you're in some sort of danger as Brad has suggested, then it's best to confront it head on." He decided right then and there that he would not let her out of his sight until the matter was resolved.

"Do you live on the Cape?" Emilia asked.

She relaxed as she listened to him ramble on about where he wanted to live then finally revealed that he lived in Fall River.

Emilia liked the sound of his voice and when he turned and looked directly into her eyes, her heart began to beat faster and she felt a warm glow all over. She couldn't remember ever being with anyone who made her feel so completely at ease. Although most people were not aware of it, she was a little self-conscious. She realized she wasn't with Dennis.

"Do you like the style of the houses on the Cape?" Emilia asked.

"I like the houses with the natural cedar shakes," he said.

"That's part of the charm surrounding the area," she agreed. "At least we know we have something in common."

The ride and the casual conversation seemed to be having a good effect. She could feel herself relaxing. If I weren't aware of our destination, I'd actually be enjoying myself she thought.

"How far is that restaurant from here?" she asked.

"It's called the Thomasville Inn and it's just up ahead," Dennis said. "I'm hungry enough to eat a horse."

"I'm a little hungry myself," Emilia agreed.

Emilia and Dennis had just finished eating when a waiter walked over to their table and told Dennis he had a phone call.

Emilia watched Dennis walk out to the lobby. She wondered who would be calling him. She didn't have to wait long.

"Who was on the phone?" Emilia asked. "Did you tell someone we would be stopping here?"

"No, I didn't," Dennis replied. "It was Brad."

"Why would he call?" Emilia asked. "We're on our way to see him now. I suppose it would be unrealistic to hope he changed his mind. Or something's come up and he doesn't have time to see us now."

"You're losing it." Dennis said. "He called to say he was arranging for someone to pick us up." He motioned for the waitress and told her they would like another cup of coffee.

"Why is he sending someone to pick us up?" she asked. "I don't understand."

"When you called Irene last night, did you tell her Brad thought you might be in some sort of danger?"

"Yes, I did," she replied. "What does that have to do with this?"

"Evidently Irene called Brad this morning and told him about someone who she thinks called the office on the pretense of making an appointment. She later realized she had been tricked into inadvertently telling them where you had gone. She was almost frantic with worry. She didn't know what to do, so she called Brad."

"Maybe Irene's imagination is working overtime," Emilia said.

"Well, Brad didn't think so after she relayed the conversation to him," Dennis said. "He called Jeremy Archer, the Chief of Police in East Sandwich, and requested an escort for us."

"Do you think that's really necessary?" she asked. She was slightly annoyed and was sure he saw it in her face. She stopped speaking when the waitress brought their coffee. "We can only hope they don't show up in a police car."

"I don't think they will," he said. "I understand Chief Archer is sending a couple of detectives. Brad is just being cautious because he is concerned."

Despite her intense sensitivity with regard to Brad's business association, she appreciated the fact that he was concerned with her personal welfare.

"I'm sorry," she said. "I do appreciate his concern." She felt that Dennis was impressed with the mature perception she showed in the matter.

"I suppose I should call Irene," Emilia said. "She's probably worried sick."

"I'm sure you have time," he said. "The phone is right around the corner from the check out."

"I'll be right back," she said. She got up and headed in the direction he had indicated.

The waitress was heating up their coffee when she came back a few minutes later and sat down. "It's a good thing I called," she said. "Irene would never forgive herself if anything happened to me because of her." Emilia sipped her coffee.

"You know, we're going to have to get this whole mess resolved," she said.

"Absolutely," Dennis agreed. "Whoever is after you may not get you this time, but they'll keep trying until they do."

"But I don't understand why someone is after me," Emilia said. "It's got me feeling jumpy and that's making me angry. Does Brad know who and why? Does it have something to do with my mother? It seems as though her death precipitated this whole thing with me. I know you'll find this hard to believe but I can't wait to see him now, if only to get answers to these questions." She looked into his eyes.

"Believe me, I can appreciate how you feel," he responded. "Brad may not have all the answers but I'm sure he'll tell you whatever he can." Dennis reached across the table and squeezed her hand. Emilia felt something similar to an electric shock when their fingers touched. She ached to have his arms around her. From what she read in his eyes, she had no doubt that's exactly what would have happened had they been alone. Instead, she received one of those dazzling smiles that left her weak in the knees.

Time seemed to stand still as they waited for the escort Brad was sending.

Emilia was the first to notice the two men as they entered the restaurant. They scanned the room until they saw Dennis and Emilia and then headed toward their table. They introduced themselves as Detectives Jacob and Stevens and showed Dennis their identification.

They explained they had been filled in on the situation and as far as they could determine everything appeared to be under control. They asked if Emilia or Dennis had noticed anything out of the ordinary. Emilia indicated everything was fine and the four of them left the restaurant and quickly walked to an unmarked police car.

"What about my car?" Dennis asked. "I hate to leave it here in the parking lot."

"Maybe we'll have someone in the area later on who can pick up your car," Detective Jacob said. "We're under orders to take both of you to Brad Owensford's residence. We don't want to do anything that might jeopardize Miss Wright's safety."

Dennis agreed since he didn't want to do anything that might harm Emilia. It was hard for him to believe they had only met yesterday. Even more difficult for him to comprehend was the realization that he had fallen in love in less time than it takes to get over a twenty-four hour virus.

The ride to East Sandwich was scenic and uneventful. Emilia was glad Chief Archer had sent an unmarked car as Dennis predicted. She discovered the only distinguishable difference between a marked and an unmarked car was on the outside. The inside was equipped with standard police communication controls. Although Detectives Jacob and Stevens gave the appearance of being very casual, she felt sure they were on alert and ready for anything suspicious.

I will be so glad when this ordeal is over she thought. Emilia tried to remain positive and keep in mind that Dennis said she would like Brad Owensford who was looking forward to their meeting. She realized Dennis knew Brad Owensford quite well since Brad had been a client of his for many years, but she still felt vulnerable.

Emilia looked over at Dennis and he put his arm around her as though he sensed her discomfort. Although she usually disliked being touched, this gesture of tenderness made her feel loved and secure and she did not pull away.

"How soon will we be there?" she asked.

"In about fifteen minutes," Dennis replied taking her hand. "Are you all right?"

"I'm all right now," she replied. She felt so comfortable with his arm around her; she didn't care how long it took to get there.

She turned and looked out the window as they turned onto a narrow dirt road with trees lining both sides. It was marked 'private' and seemed to be very remote with nothing visible in the distance except more trees.

"How far back from the road is Brad's house?" Emilia asked.

"It's probably two or three miles," Dennis replied. "His house used to be the Coast Guard headquarters for the area. It stands on a bluff overlooking Cape Cod Bay and a private beach. The house has been enlarged and completely remodeled, including a security system that would make Fort Knox envious." He pointed out the window. "Look, it's just coming into view."

Emilia caught her breath at the sight. Although the house was beautiful, it was the background that made her audibly gasp. Something about the way the sky looked with all those billowy white clouds, presenting a semblance of stretching out as far as the eye could see, with the sun's rays filtering through onto this charming Cape Cod house. An artist would be tempted to sell his soul for the chance to paint a scene like this she thought.

"Oh, Denny, it's just beautiful," Emilia exclaimed.

"You think this is something," Dennis told her. "Wait until you see the view from inside."

Emilia and Dennis got out of the car, thanked the two detectives and started for the front door. Emilia was still a little apprehensive but with Dennis at her side holding her hand, she felt reassured that everything would be all right.

~ SIX ~

Emilia saw someone at the front window as she and Dennis started up the walk toward the front door. An older man opened the door before Dennis had a chance to ring the bell. Emilia remembered seeing a photograph of her mother and this man among her mother's personal belongings. At the time, she wondered who he was. Although he was much younger in the photograph, Emilia knew this had to be Brad Owensford. He was handsome in the photograph, and still was. The years had been good to him. He was very distinguished looking and, although his hair was almost white, he appeared much younger than he was. He had the physique of a man in his forties. He was tall, relatively thin, and had extraordinary bluish-gray eyes.

"Denny, come in," he said. "And this must be Emilia."

"How do you do, Mr. Owensford," she said. "Your house is beautiful." She looked around as they stepped inside.

"Thank you, Emilia," he replied. "Please call me Brad. Later on, I'll show you the whole house and we can take a walk down to the beach. The sandbar should be up right after lunch. I often walk on the sandbar and look for shells for relaxation."

"I'd love that," Emilia said. "You'll come, too, won't you Denny?"

"I wouldn't miss it," he chuckled. "I can't think of anything better than walking in your bare feet on a sandbar."

Emilia laughed at this projected image. She heard the tenseness in her voice and wondered if they noticed.

"Let's go sit in the living room," Brad said. "We can get acquainted while lunch is being prepared. Afterwards, we'll go down to the beach."

The living room faced the ocean as well as the front of the house. The back wall facing the ocean was one huge window from the ceiling almost to the floor. As Emilia looked out, the ocean appeared to have no end. The view was spectacular, especially the waves as they crashed against the large stone barrier on the beach. She could just imagine what the sunrise was like.

Although the room was spacious, it had the look of a cottage and was done in a country motif. There were a few scattered throw rugs on a beautifully polished hardwood floor. The broad fireplace located on the side wall held several logs all ready to be lit.

Emilia noticed a large portrait of her mother hung over the fireplace. She walked over to look at it. "That's a wonderful likeness," she said. "I have a lot of pictures of my mother when she was younger." She looked at Brad and saw the way his eyes softened as he looked at the portrait. She didn't doubt for one minute that he had loved her.

"Please sit down," Brad said. The comfortable looking furniture was situated near the fireplace and Emilia and Dennis sat on the couch facing the window with the view of the ocean. "Can I get you something to drink while we're waiting for our lunch?"

When Emilia and Dennis both declined, Brad walked over and sat down in one of the chairs opposite them. Emilia put her purse down on the coffee table that was situated between the couch and the two chairs.

"I understand you teach smoking cessation," Brad said. "Do you enjoy your work?"

"Yes, I do," Emilia replied. "It's interesting as well as very satisfying. It gives me an opportunity to meet and interact with people from all walks of life. I feel very fortunate to be able to contribute something which will benefit the community."

"I can relate to that," Brad said. "I also feel privileged to be in a position to do that, at least on a personal level. On the other hand, a great deal of my money is being used to support an organization which represents a power bent on the destruction of our country. I have no choice but to continue to support it."

Emilia sensed the agony he felt as he told her this. Dennis was right about the way she would feel when she met him. She liked him immensely. He was considerate, soft spoken and such a gentleman. But there was something more. It was the way he looked at her. Perhaps I remind him of my mother she thought. It was easy now to believe her mother loved him. In addition to being extremely handsome, he projected such unfeigned refinement and culture you couldn't help but respect and like him.

"I don't understand," Emilia said. "Why must you support it? Especially when you know their agenda could lead to the destruction of our country."

"Yes, I do know that," Brad said. "How do you think I feel when I see what my money is sponsoring? It looks like I endorse racism, protection of the Ku Klux Klan, Nazi organizations, and dozens of other anti-American organizations. My money is used to protect their freedom of speech."

Emilia could see that Brad was becoming more emotional as he spoke. The anger he felt was unmistakable. He got up and paced the room as he continued. "I wonder what our World War II veterans think about protecting their freedom of speech? They have attacked religion, our Public School System, our Justice Department, etc., etc, etc."

Emilia understood now why Dennis had asked her to give Brad the benefit of the doubt. It was obvious he was not supporting the APLA by choice. She looked at Dennis and indicated with a nod that she understood now what he had been trying to tell her.

"I'm so sorry, Brad," she said. "Things are not always what they seem, and in the future I will not be judgmental without knowing all the facts. But what part do I play in all this?" She watched Brad come back across the room and sit down in his chair.

"I'll try to answer your question as simply as I can," he replied. "It started a long time ago with your mother. They promised she would come to no harm as long as I supported their cause. I loved your mother, which left me no choice at all."

"May I ask you something? Why didn't you and my mother marry? It's hard for me to believe it was because she wouldn't turn Catholic." Dennis got up and Emilia watched him as he walked over to the window and stood looking out at the ocean.

"That's what everyone thought," Brad answered. "My parents made such a fuss, I did ask Katherine if she would consider turning Catholic. She told me she could not embrace a religion unless she could accept all its teachings, not even for me."

"That sounds exactly like my mother," Emilia said. She leaned back on the pillows and crossed her legs as Brad continued.

"I respected and loved her even more for her integrity," he said. "My parents, thinking time would change the way we felt about each other, sent me to Europe on business. I guess they never heard the axiom that absence makes the heart grow fonder. Katherine was away when I left, so I wrote a note and attached it to the pin you now have and gave it to my brother to give to her when she returned. In the note I explained that I was just humoring my parents who promised, if we still felt the same way when I returned, not to stand in our way. I professed my love for her and asked her to wait for me." Emilia heard the sadness in his voice and saw the heartache in his face even though it had happened many years ago.

"Then if she loved you, I don't understand why she didn't wait," Emilia said. "Did you ever see her again?"

"No, I never did," Brad softly replied. "But I never stopped loving her." Emilia heard his voice break and his face twisted in remembered pain. She waited for him to regain his composure before she spoke.

"Didn't you even ask her why she didn't wait?" Emilia asked.

"No, I didn't. When I came back she had already married your father," he replied. "I was heartbroken, of course, and knowing why she didn't wait would have been irrelevant in any case." Emilia saw Dennis turn around and look to see if she needed him. She could feel the tears sting her eyes as he walked back over and sat down on the couch beside her.

"But they knew you still loved her and would not knowingly allow any harm to come to her," Emilia said. "So all these years they have been extorting money from you. But now the threat is no longer valid and you've got to put a stop to it." Emilia could feel herself becoming excited.

"Denny, isn't there some legal way to stop this?" Emilia asked.

"I'm afraid there's a little more to it," Brad said. "They are now threatening to harm you. That's why I wanted you here. So we could meet and determine how best to proceed in order to get it resolved without jeopardizing your safety." She shivered with fear when he spoke of this actual threat to harm her. Dennis felt it and put his arm around her.

"But that's absurd," Emilia exclaimed. "It was my mother you loved, not me."

Then she remembered wondering about the way he looked at her when they first arrived. It was his eyes. She realized his eyes looked exactly like hers, even down to the bluish-gray color. And the emotion she saw in them was not love for her mother, but love for her. She wanted to ask him much more but just then, his housekeeper entered the room and announced that lunch was ready. It would have to wait.

Emilia knew they would be eating outdoors on the deck. She heard Brad instruct his housekeeper of that shortly after their arrival.

As they went through the dining room, Emilia noticed it, too, was done in a country motif similar to that found in the living room. The furniture was magnificent and appeared to be solid oak, matching the polished hardwood floor. As in the living room, the wall facing the ocean was all windows and included a sliding glass door, which opened onto the deck. I could get used to this in no time at all, she thought.

They went through the sliding glass doors onto a large deck that ran the entire length of the back of the house. There was a large round table and six chairs where the housekeeper had already laid out their lunch. This was by the doors. At the other end of the deck she saw a glider and several deck chairs. There were several small tables and many plants, both hanging and in large planter boxes built along the edge of the deck. It was a very attractive setting.

"Please sit down," Brad said. "Let's eat our lunch."

Emilia saw they were having a chicken pasta salad served on a half cantaloupe. There were hot rolls and butter and iced tea to drink.

"You don't have to coax me," she said. "The sea air always gives me an appetite." The three of them sat down to eat lunch. "This salad is delicious, Emilia said. "In fact, everything tastes so good. It's perfect for a hot afternoon."

"I'm glad you like it," Brad said. "I was hoping the rain would hold off so we could eat out here on the deck. There's always a nice breeze from the ocean. Air conditioning is nice but it can't take the place of good fresh salt-water air."

"It also makes you sleep like a log," Dennis said. "I have to set my alarm when I've been out here." Emilia passed Dennis another roll.

"It must be wonderful to live next to the ocean," Emilia said. She leaned back in her chair and sipped her iced tea.

"Yes, it is," Brad replied. "I hope you'll be moving here soon, Denny. I have a piece of property about a half mile up the beach I'd be willing to sell if you're interested."

"I sure would be," Dennis exclaimed. "In fact, I'm flattered. I know you bought everything up around here to ensure your privacy." Dennis wiped his mouth on his napkin and put it on his plate. Emilia thought how relaxed he looked as he leaned back in his chair.

"Do you like the Cape, Emilia?" Brad asked. "I know Katherine grew up on the Cape but when she married your father, they moved to Plymouth. Didn't he sell office furniture for a manufacturer located there?"

"Yes, he did," she replied. "I love the Cape. As I was telling Dennis on the way over, Sandwich is one of my favorite towns."

As they finished their lunch, Emilia marveled at the congeniality that existed between them. It far exceeded her expectations.

After the dishes were cleared away, Emilia asked Brad if they could remain out on the deck to continue their discussion.

"It's all right with me," Brad said.

"Sounds good to me," Dennis agreed.

"Could we start where we left off?" Emilia asked. "Why would they think you'd cooperate with them if they threatened to harm me?" I really have to know the answer to that one she thought.

"I'm not sure. Maybe they think I wouldn't want to feel responsible if anything happened to Katherine's daughter," Brad replied. Emilia saw him look at her to see if she would buy that explanation. He didn't have to wait long for her reaction.

"I don't think that's even a possibility since they know how you feel about them. I think they realize they've lost their hold on you and now they are just bluffing. Once they understand you know this, that will be the end of it."

"I wouldn't be too hasty, Emilia," Dennis said. "You may be jumping to conclusions."

"I don't think so," she replied. "There is no reason to believe I am in serious danger because I happen to be Katherine's daughter. In fact, I should go home and stop letting my imagination run away with me. Not that I'm sorry I came to visit. I wouldn't have missed it for the world," she said sarcastically.

"You can't go home," Dennis said in a harsh tone. "You are still in danger" Emilia watched him practically jump to his feet with a scowl on his face. She knew he was clearly annoyed as he shot her an angry glance.

"Then there must be something more you're not telling me," she responded. "What you're trying to make me believe doesn't make any sense. And don't speak to me again in that tone of voice." Emilia could see that Brad was also getting upset.

"Brad, you've got to tell her," Dennis begged.

"Don't bother, I already know." Emilia looked into the eyes so like her own. "You're my father, aren't you?"

Emilia saw Brad and Dennis look at her in disbelief. They were so concerned with the most suitable course to announce this news, it never occurred to them that she already suspected she was Brad's daughter. When the look of disbelief turned to one of relief she knew the answer before Brad spoke.

"Yes, I am," Brad said. "I've wanted to tell you for a long time but didn't think you would believe me."

"I don't think I would have if you had tried to tell me before we'd met." Emilia replied. She could feel the hot tears in her eyes spill over and run down her cheeks as she continued. "Although there were times during the years when I had doubts that my dad was really my biological father, the one most compelling instance happened shortly after my mother's death as I was going through her papers." Emilia left out a sob, which brought Dennis and Brad both to her side. She realized how much they both cared for her.

"I'm sorry I lost my temper," Dennis said. "Please forgive me."

Brad put his arm around her and gave her his handkerchief.

"I'm all right now," she said. "Please let me finish."

Dennis and Brad went back to their chairs and sat down.

"I came across their marriage certificate and found that someone had changed the date. At the time, I only suspected that my mother was pregnant before they got married. But after I found out about you, I wondered if that was all there was to it. Then I met you and it was your eyes that gave me the answer. Although I can accept all this logically, it's going to take a while to really sink in." Emilia smiled at them even though the tears continued to flow.

Emilia saw Dennis look at her and then at Brad.

"What's the matter," she asked. Emilia wiped away the tears and blew her nose.

"I can't believe I didn't notice it when I saw the two of you together," Dennis replied. "You and Brad have identical looking eyes with that same characteristic inability to conceal your emotions. I'm glad it's out in the open. Now you two can get to know each other."

"There's nothing I'd like better," Brad said. "But first, I think we better concentrate on Emilia's safety."

"Didn't you tell me Chief Archer was coming over later?" Dennis asked. "You said he had to fill out an official report about the escort this morning. Maybe we should wait until he gets here to continue with this."

"I think Dennis is right," Emilia said. "We don't even know what we're up against yet."

"He might be just what we need," Brad agreed. "Someone who is not personally involved would tend to be more objective. I know we can trust Chief Archer to be discreet. I'll call and ask him to come over now if he's free."

- SEVEN -

When Brad left to telephone Chief Archer, Dennis and Emilia left the table and went to stand at the railing on the deck. Emilia thought that the ocean under the sun's rays would have looked like glass had it not been for the ripples of the tide as it came to shore. Trouble seemed a million miles away in this scenario.

"What are you thinking about?" Dennis asked.

"I was thinking about my mother and dad," Emilia replied. "Finding out Brad is my biological father doesn't change the way I feel about them. I was remembering some of the things that stand out and made a difference for some unknown reason. Like the time my dad bought me my first two-wheeled bike and the cape and hat outfit I just had to have, even though my mother said we couldn't afford it."

"It sounds to me like you had some pretty terrific parents," Dennis said.

"Yes, I did," she said. "Some things are so vivid. I remember how hard my mother and I laughed when my dad rode that bike down a hill, which was more like the side of a mountain, to make sure it was safe before I rode it."

Emilia relaxed as she talked about her parents. She was glad they took a break from the problem at hand. She was very upset a short while ago and Dennis certainly didn't help any when he lost his temper. She knew it was because he was worried about her.

"There were also the dancing and singing lessons I had to have," she said. "They did their best to give me the material things that all kids want. Since I was an only child, they were financially able to do it."

"I think we all have memories like that," Dennis said. "We have a tendency to lose sight of it over the years."

"You're right about that," Emilia said. "More important than material things, they made sure I attended Sunday School and Church, which instilled in me a moral and ethical background. I sometimes wonder how people without a belief in God are able to survive the adversities in life."

"I've wondered that myself," Dennis said.

Emilia and Dennis walked to the other end of the deck and looked down at the beach below. She loved to listen to the sound of the ocean waves as they rolled in toward the shore. It was fascinating to see a huge wave end up as a puddle of foam when it hit the sand.

"Over the years, they taught me to put things in the proper perspective."

"Such as?" he asked.

"Such as, you don't always win because you're right, that beauty is only skin deep, you should do your best to be modest and reserved, that people swear because they have an undeveloped vocabulary, and if you don't have something nice to say about a person, don't say anything at all. In this day and age, that would most assuredly be considered square."

Dennis laughed. "I'm afraid you're right about that."

"There was no trace of bigotry in either of them," she said. "I grew up to believe that one man was no better than another. Also, no job was menial as long as it was done well. Last, but not least, never look down your nose at someone less fortunate than yourself."

"I think they did a wonderful job with you," Dennis said.

"I'm sorry," she said. "I've been going on and on. I should take a break and come up for air once in a while."

"That's all right," Dennis said. "It's just nerves. You've been under quite a strain through all this. I think you've held up better than most and your parents would be proud of you."

"Thanks," Emilia said. "I'm awfully glad you're in my corner."

"I'm also in your corner," Brad said as he came out on the deck. "I'm sure you already know that." Emilia and Dennis turned and saw Brad coming to rejoin them. She thought she heard the sliding door open and close. He had a glass of iced tea and asked if they would like something to drink. Emilia didn't want anything but Dennis said he would join him. Emilia and Dennis sat down at the table while Brad went to get Dennis his tea.

"Were you able to get through to Chief Archer," she asked as he gave Dennis his drink and sat down with them.

"Yes, I did," Brad replied. "He said he could come right over. He should be here in about ten minutes."

"Are you going to tell him everything you told us?" she asked.

"I think we'll have to give him all the facts if we want him to effectively be of help to us," Brad replied. "I think we're lucky he's offered his help. His expertise in police work is well known."

"Yes, it is," Dennis said. "His reputation is well known throughout the state of Massachusetts. He's given me help on a few tough cases over the years."

When Chief Archer arrived, they went back to the living room and sat down. Emilia sensed that he was very perceptive to the somewhat tense atmosphere. She was aware that, even though it wasn't meant to be obvious, he thoroughly scrutinized each one of them. She saw him nod as he recognized Dennis. Emilia and Dennis sat on the sofa and Brad and Chief Archer sat on the two chairs opposite them. Dennis got a coaster and put his drink down on the coffee table between them.

"Chief," Brad said. "I'd like to introduce my daughter, Emilia Wright."

"How do you do." Chief Archer said. "I wasn't aware Mr. Owensford had a daughter, and such a lovely one at that."

"Thank you. I'm glad to meet you," Emilia replied.

"And I think you already know Dennis McClelland," Brad said.

"Yes, I do," Chief Archer said. "Nice to see you again Mr. McClelland. I don't know what's up, but I'm here to help in any way I can."

"Thanks," Brad said. "I appreciate that. Can I get you something to drink before we get started."

"No, thank you," he said. "Suppose you tell me what this is all about."

Emilia watched the shocked look on his face as Brad told him about being blackmailed to the tune of millions of dollars for over forty years. When he told him he knew the money was being used to support the APLA, Chief Archer looked absolutely horrified.

"I don't understand," he interrupted. "What possible reason could you have for going along with that?"

"I had no choice," Brad said and took a long gulp of his drink. "They threatened to harm Katherine, whom I loved very much, even though she married someone else and moved from the Cape."

"Who is Katherine and where is she now?" Chief Archer asked.

"Katherine was Emilia's mother," Brad replied. "She died about two months ago. That's her portrait hanging over the fireplace." Brad got up and walked over to look up at the portrait. "There's an explanation for why she married someone else and if you think it's important we can go into it later. Someone knew even before I did, that Katherine's child, Emilia, was my daughter."

Emilia watched Brad walk to the other side of the room and refill his glass. "That information was relayed a couple years later, knowing it would serve to reinforce the original threat."

"Mr. Owensford, do you know the blackmailer's identity?" Chief Archer asked.

"No, I don't," Brad replied as he sat down in his chair. "Before Katherine died, she sent me a pin I once gave her. I believe that was her way of asking me to help Emilia and keep her safe. I wasn't aware she knew about the threat. She must have realized I knew Emilia was my daughter. That's when I decided to try and get Emilia to come here and see if there wasn't some way I could put an end to this whole thing."

Emilia wondered why her mother never told her about this. Perhaps she was afraid and didn't want me to get involved she thought. Or she realized I was better off not knowing. Emilia got up and walked over to the fireplace to look again at the portrait. "I sure gave him a hard time about coming," Emilia said as she walked back and sat down again on the sofa. "As if he needed any more stress in his life. I hope you'll forgive me, Brad, because I didn't have any idea then."

"There's nothing to forgive," Brad said. "You had no way of knowing. You are the innocent one in this whole mess. The only good thing to come out of it."

Emilia watched as Chief Archer got up, stretched and walked over to look out the window at the ocean.

"Mr. Owensford, you sure know how to open up a can of worms," he said. "We'll have to do a complete investigation before deciding on the best course of action."

"I know," Brad said. "I'm sorry to drop this bombshell right in your lap. My primary concern is Emilia's safety."

"I can appreciate that," Chief Archer said. He left the window and returned to his chair. "Let's look at the facts we do know."

Emilia listened carefully as he continued.

"There's a powerful and corrupt organization out there that your money has been supporting for the past forty years. They will not be pleased to hear that you've decided to withdraw your support. In fact, I'd be willing to wager they will do whatever it takes to see that it doesn't happen."

"I agree," Dennis said. "I think the first order of business should be to determine who is behind this plot. I think it would have to be someone eaten up with hate after all these years."

Emilia couldn't imagine anyone hating Brad with such a vengeance. It would take a vicious person to persecute someone for over forty years she thought. When she leaned forward to cross her legs, she felt the tight muscles in her shoulders and realized how stiff she was holding herself. She laid her hands in her lap, took a deep breath and purposely willed herself to relax.

"Mr. Owensford, can you think of anyone who might feel they have a legitimate reason to hate you?" Chief Archer asked. "Anyone at all? Someone who might be retaliating for some perceived wrong they believe you did them."

"No, not really," Brad replied.

"Did I detect a slight hesitation on your part?" Emilia asked. "Who were you just thinking of?"

"I was thinking of my brother Jeff," Brad said. "He always thought I deliberately set out to take Katherine away from him. Shortly after that happened, my father disinherited him and changed his will. I assumed it was because of Jeff's behavior toward me with regard to Katherine. My father died a few years later and left his entire estate to me."

"How did your brother react when this happened?" Emilia asked.

"He was angry and it caused a rift between us which exists to this day. I thought he would eventually get over it and we could at least be cordial but it never happened. I was willing to forget the past, and I did make sure he received enough money to live on comfortably for the rest of his life. He probably doesn't even need it. I understand he's a very successful investment broker."

"So you don't think he has anything to do with this?" Chief Archer asked.

"I'm probably the last thing on his mind," Brad replied. "I know he got married shortly after going to Chicago. In fact, his daughter lives here on the Cape in the town of Dennis. Her name is Joyce Hanson and I do see her from time to time. She is my niece, after all, and we are on the best of terms."

"Can you think of anyone else?" Chief Archer asked. "Anyone at all who might have known about Katherine and Emilia besides your brother?"

"It's possible that Robert Wright might have known," Brad said. "What do you think Emilia? Do you recall anything that might indicate whether he did or not?"

Emilia got up and walked back to the fireplace. "I really don't," she said. "I never heard either of them mention it. I can only tell you they appeared to be very compatible."

"It's kind of irrelevant anyway," Dennis said. "Emilia's dad died two years ago."

"That's true," Brad said. He got up and joined Emilia in front of the fireplace.

"Can't you think of anyone else who might have known?" she asked. "Think about it."

Emilia watched Brad rub his forehead as he tried to remember something he may have overlooked.

"I'm sorry," Brad said. "I can't think of anyone else who could possibly have known."

"Well, let's forget that for now," Emilia said. "We better concentrate on what to do for the present."

"That makes sense," Dennis said. "I don't think Emilia should go anywhere alone. I've already told her I won't leave her until this is over."

"How about hiring some bodyguards?" Emilia asked.

"That's exactly what I had in mind," Chief Archer replied. "We know this is a serious threat, not fun and games."

"I'd pay handsomely for professional people who have been well trained," Brad said. "Maybe former FBI or Secret Service."

"I think I could arrange for that," Chief Archer said. "We have a list of personnel who are available for special assignments. It may take a day or two to communicate and line up the individuals you'll choose. In the meantime, I think it's best that Emilia stay here with you. I'll assign a couple of detectives to your surveillance. Since you recently installed the best security system on the market, I don't think we have to worry about anyone breaking in."

"We already have Dennis," Emilia said. "He is staying here too." She walked over to the window. "I hadn't planned on staying here that long, but if you think it's necessary, I'll call my secretary and let her know I won't be back for a few days."

"Please don't tell her anything else," Chief Archer said.

"Oh, I won't," Emilia replied as she walked back to the sofa and sat down. "I realize it's best to keep everything as confidential as possible. Things have a way of leaking out."

"Yes, they do," he said. "We don't want to give them the advantage of knowing what our next move will be."

"That's good advice," Brad said. "Sometimes without meaning to, we inadvertently let things slip."

"I think I'll take off now and get started on this," Chief Archer said as he stood up and straightened his jacket. Brad left the fireplace to walk him to the door.

"Thanks for coming," Brad said as they shook hands.

"Take care," Chief Archer said. "I'll give you a call later."

Emilia heard Brad tell his housekeeper that she and Dennis would be staying for dinner and overnight. In a way, she was glad. After all the talk about her being in danger, she felt a little more secure right here. At least, until she sorted things out for herself and decided what she wanted to do.

"How about our walk on the beach?" Brad asked as he came back into the living room.

Emilia and Dennis both jumped up ready to go.

"Do you think it's OK?" Dennis asked.

"Yes, I certainly do," Brad replied.

"I think we could use a little relaxation," Emilia said. "Exercise is one of the best things for stress. I can honestly say, I, for one, am all stressed out."

"Then let's go," Dennis said.

"I think I'll call Irene first before I forget," Emilia said. "She's probably expecting a call about now. Then there will be no need to hurry back."

"That's better yet," Dennis said.

Emilia told Dennis and Brad to go on ahead while she called Irene. She was on the phone with Irene for about five minutes and then went outside in search of Dennis and Brad. She saw them waiting for her by the steps leading down from the deck. It was breezy and the sky was a little cloudy as they headed down to the beach. Emilia noticed that the sandbar was almost up. They were right on time.

When they got down to the beach, Dennis suddenly stopped.

"Aren't we going to take off our shoes and socks before we hit the sandbar?" he asked in a teasing way. "Or are you two much too conservative for that?"

"I've been called worse," Brad countered. "But I do believe I'll join you. How about you, Emilia?"

Emilia laughed. "It looks like I have no choice," she said. "I'll have to join you."

As they neared the shoreline, the beach was a little rocky. They carefully picked their way out into the water and over the stones until they reached the sandbar. Dennis was right she thought. It was wonderful walking on the sandbar in your bare feet. Unlike the sand on the beach, which was dry and hot and squished up between your toes, the sand on the sandbar was wet and cool and smooth as velvet. It was one of the larger sandbars and the three of them separated and began looking for shells, moving the sand and bending over to examine every fragment of shell they uncovered to see if it was broken or intact. As the tension buildup of the day drained away, she remembered Brad saying how relaxing this was for him. At this moment in time, she couldn't be happier.

"Want to take a walk up the beach?" Brad called to her. "There's an area posted as a preserve for the sandpiper, one of our endangered species. Sometimes you can catch a peek at them, but you have to be careful not to get too close or they might come after you." Emilia walked over to see where he was pointing.

"Do you think it's OK?" Dennis asked as he came over to join them.

"Maybe you're right," Brad said. "I wasn't thinking."

"Oh, come on," Emilia started walking. "I have no intention of living the rest of my life looking over my shoulder for unseen assailants."

Emilia saw Dennis shake his head in exasperation. She hoped he was not getting angry again. She took a good look at him but saw only concern.

"I'm not suggesting you do that for the rest of your life," Dennis replied. "Just until we have your bodyguards in place. I don't want anything to happen to you."

"Nor do I," Brad agreed. "I'm afraid you're outnumbered."

"OK," Emilia said. "I know when to give up."

Just then, they noticed the two men standing up on the deck watching them.

"Can you see who it is?" Brad asked.

Emilia put her hand up to shade her eyes from the light. "Yes, It's the two detectives who escorted us here this morning."

"I guess Chief Archer sent them for Emilia's protection until she has her own bodyguards. I'll go up and show them around the place. You two can stay down here for a while if you like. Dinner won't be ready yet." The three of them sat down on the beach and put their shoes back on.

"Thanks," Emilia said as Brad headed for the steps. She looked at Dennis and smiled. "Would you like to walk on the beach a little longer?"

"If you want to," he replied. He took her hand and they walked up the beach along the shoreline.

"This is nice," Emilia said. "It's so peaceful and therapeutic. It's a good way to block everything out." Emilia stopped and pointed. "Oh, look, there's a sea gull. I love to watch them. Did you ever see how they sit on top of the poles at the dock? My dad said they are filthy birds but I don't care. To me, they are beautiful."

"I'm glad you're staying here with Brad tonight," Dennis said as they began to walk again. "At least I'll be able to get a good night's sleep."

"Aren't you staying, too?" Emilia asked. "Remember, you did promise not to leave me."

"I know I did," Dennis said. "I wanted to give you and Brad a little time alone to get acquainted."

"I'd rather you stayed," she replied. "Brad and I will have all the time in the world to get acquainted when this is all over."

"I'll do whatever you want," Dennis said. "You must know how I feel about you."

Emilia stopped walking and turned to look up into his eyes. "Yes, I think I do," she said. "And I feel the same. But I don't want you to get involved in this situation. It isn't fair to you. Maybe when all this is over . . . . ."

She never got a chance to finish her argument. Dennis put his arms around her and pulled her close, holding her so tight she was breathless. Then he caressed her, and gently kissed her cheeks, her eyes and at long last, her lips. Emilia hungrily responded and as she arched her body toward him, his kisses grew hard and more passionate.

"I better stop," he whispered in her ear. "I'll need to take a swim in the ocean to cool off."

Emilia wondered how far she would have let him go if he had not stopped. As she felt him reluctantly pull away from her, she knew she was falling in love.

"I've wanted to do that all day," he said. "And I don't want to hear anymore about me not getting involved. I am already involved . . . . .I love you."

Emilia and Dennis had their arms around each other as they walked back toward the house. Emilia saw Brad on the deck watching them as they reached the steps. She noticed his smile as they came up on the deck and sensed that he was pleased by what she was sure he had witnessed on the beach below.

"Did you two have a nice walk?" Brad asked.

"Yes, we did," Emilia replied. "If you and Dennis don't mind, I think I'll go upstairs and take a shower and change clothes before dinner."

"Take your time," Brad said. "It won't be ready for a while."

"Do you think I'd have time to take a run over to the Sandwich Police Station before dinner?" Dennis asked. "Maybe I can help Chief Archer scan the personnel files for potential bodyguards for Emilia."

"You probably have about two hours," Brad said. "I'm going to lay down out here on the glider for a while and relax. I'll see you when you get back."

Dennis got to the police station in about fifteen minutes and told the desk sergeant he would like to see Chief Archer. Dennis saw the look of surprise on the Chief's face as he came out of his office.

"I came down to see if I could be of any help," Dennis said. "You mentioned something about searching through personnel files and I thought maybe you could use some help."

"Yes, I could," Chief Archer said. "To be truthful, I haven't even started yet. I had company waiting to see me when I got back."

"Anybody I know?" Dennis asked.

"No," Chief Archer replied. "But they were here concerning Brad and Emilia. By the way, what I'm about to tell you is strictly confidential."

"I understand," Dennis said. "You don't have to worry about me. I wouldn't do anything to jeopardize Emilia's safety."

"My company was the FBI, specifically Agents Lawson and Bradley," Chief Archer said. "They were told I was about to get involved in a case that they've had under surveillance for quite some time, namely Brad Owensford and the APLA. They politely told me 'hands off'."

"Can they really stop you from getting involved?" Dennis asked.

"I don't think so," Chief Archer said. "They probably want to make sure we don't undermine any progress they've made so far. They weren't at liberty to give me any additional information."

"Did you offer your assistance in their investigation?" Dennis asked.

"I did," Chief Archer said. "I told them Mr. Owensford is a friend. They said they would get back to me."

Dennis was beginning to appreciate the magnitude of the trouble Brad was in. Since he was a private investigator, he was free to do whatever investigation he felt was necessary to get to the bottom of this. Nobody was going to tell him to stay out of it. Not when it meant Emilia might end up getting hurt. The first order of business after the bodyguards were in place would be to find out who was blackmailing Brad.

"Well, how about showing me where those files are and I'll start scanning them," Dennis said. He was still in the computer room when the desk sergeant came into the room and told him he had a phone call. Now who would be calling me here he wondered? When he picked up the phone and heard Emilia's voice, he looked at his watch and realized they must be waiting dinner for him. He told her he had completely lost track of time but he would be there in fifteen minutes. He took the list of names he selected from the personnel files, wrote a note asking Chief Archer to please make further inquiries, and dropped it off on the sergeant's desk on his way out.

- *EIGHT* -

Jeff Owensford hurried into his office about 1:00 p.m., slamming the door behind him. He was listed as an investment broker. If anyone actually inquired after his services, they were informed he was not accepting any new clients at this particular time. In reality, Jeff Owensford was a silent partner of the Chief Executive Officer of the American Personal Liberties Association. His association with the APLA began many years ago when he left East Sandwich. He worked his way up into the top echelon of the organization very quickly.

"Are there any messages?" Jeff asked the receptionist in the outer office.

"Paul Freedman called," she said. "He said it was urgent and he'd like you to call him as soon as possible."

"Where is he now?" he asked. "Did he leave a number?"

"He said he was on his way home for lunch," she replied.

"Well, place the call and buzz me when you have him on the line," he said.

Jeff figured something must have gone wrong. Paul seldom called him at his office. How typical of Paul to call with an urgent matter and then go home for lunch. Jeff could become irritated at the sight of Paul. He only kept him around as a precaution in case he should someday regain his memory. He couldn't afford to have that happen.

He paid someone anonymously years ago to get rid of Paul, but the job was bungled. He found Paul wandering the streets close to death. He should have left him to die. Instead, he took him to the hospital hoping he would die there. Somehow, he made a miraculous recovery except for his memory, which never came back. The blunt force to his head left him with amnesia, which the hospital said might be temporary. Jeff often wondered what Paul's reaction would be if he found out Jeff was responsible for his condition.

As it turned out, Paul became a valuable asset to Jeff. He was intensely loyal because of the debt he felt he owed Jeff for saving his life. Jeff took advantage of that and made Paul an employee.

Jeff knew Paul didn't condone the philosophy of the APLA and didn't particularly care for some of the controversial assignments he received. In spite of that, he continued to do whatever Jeff needed done, including the hiring of two unsavory characters, named Jake Powell and Carl Matthews, for the surveillance of Emilia Wright shortly after her mother's death. Perhaps Paul's call has something to do with that Jeff thought.

The receptionist knocked and said, "Paul Freedman is on the line, Mr. Owensford."

"Hello, Paul," Jeff said. "What's up? You don't usually call me here."

"I wanted to keep you abreast of what's happened with Emilia Wright," Paul replied. "The two men we hired followed her every day and submitted daily reports. They noted nothing out of the ordinary until a few days ago."

"What happened then?" Jeff asked. He glanced through his mail while he listened to Paul.

"She had a private investigator named Dennis McClelland visit her office. He was there about a half-hour. He also went to her apartment that evening. Then early yesterday morning, Dennis McClelland picked her up and they drove out of town. Jake Powell found out that Dennis McClelland works for your brother and he was taking Emilia to Brad's house on the Cape. They are at his house right now. Powell called this morning for further instructions."

"That's not good," Jeff said. "I'm afraid we're going to have to put her out of circulation for a while." Jeff heard

Paul gasp. "I don't want her hurt he quickly added, just out of circulation."
"How do you want them to handle it?" Paul asked. Jeff heard the nervous tremor in Paul's voice and knew this whole matter concerning Emilia frightened him. What a spineless specimen he is Jeff thought.
"Let me think for a minute," Jeff replied. He put down the phone, got up and walked around his desk to look out the window while he wrestled with the problem. He walked back to the desk and sat down. He realized he'd have to soft pedal it with Paul.
"First, I want them to watch the house," Jeff said. "Tell them there's nothing they can do while she's in the house. Brad had one of the best security systems on the market installed when he built the place. But she may take a walk on the beach or go into town and they should wait until they get a chance to take her by surprise. I definitely want her out of circulation, the sooner the better. I'm not interested in Brad or this McClelland, just Emilia. After they have her, tell them to take her to my boat on the canal. I want to be informed as soon as it's over."
"OK," Paul said. "And I better warn them she's not to be hurt." Jeff knew better than to try and argue Paul out of that. He knew Paul couldn't understand how he could treat his own niece this way. Paul couldn't possibly understand the way he felt about Brad.
After Jeff hung up the phone, he lit a cigarette and leaned back in his chair and thought about Brad. He hated him so much he could taste it. He couldn't remember exactly when it started, probably when they were kids. Brad was always the well-behaved one, while he was the one the teachers called home about. Jeff is a maverick they said. The school recommended a complete physical evaluation. His parents refused and denied there was anything wrong with him. After all, what would their friends think? Jeff took a long drag on his cigarette.

He recalled that Brad had many friends and was involved in all sorts of school activities. Jeff preferred to be alone and spent hours in his room. When the school persisted in their recommendation for an evaluation, his parents insisted he was just shy. He knew himself it was more than shyness. As he grew older, he realized he lacked certain feelings that everyone else had. He felt absolutely no compassion and he couldn't remember ever feeling responsible or being sorry for anything. He never felt a pang of conscience. Not having a conscience is probably what got me where I am today he thought as he blew a smoke ring and watched it break up. He remembered being unable to control his hostility, losing his temper frequently, and claiming that others were plotting against him.

His parents finally admitted there was a problem and took him for a complete physical evaluation. He was present when they saw the doctor about a week later. The results of the tests were inconclusive. The doctor said his symptoms could be of a schizophrenic nature, but only time would tell whether it was true schizophrenia or some sort of delusional disorder that he would outgrow. In the meantime, he gave them medication, which would keep him under control.

Jeff remembered feeling so alone and out of it. He never realized back then that it was because of the medication. And he hated Brad with a vengeance as though he were responsible for the whole thing. Jeff ground out his cigarette in the ashtray.

Over the years and with a great deal of effort, he became very adept at hiding his emotions and interacting socially.

If it hadn't been for Brad, he felt certain he and Katherine would have gotten married. He met Katherine first. In fact, it was he who introduced her to Brad. A few months later, she rejected him for Brad. He was convinced Brad had deliberately set out to steal Katherine from him.

He never forgave him for that, even though he saw to it that Brad never married Katherine either.

The fact that Brad inherited everything when their father died made matters even worse. He no longer hated Brad. He despised him. He vowed to do everything in his power to make Brad's life a living Hell. He completely rejected every overture at reconciliation that Brad made over the years.

Jeff was so deep in thought that he literally jumped when the buzzer sounded on the intercom.

"Yes," he answered.

"Your long-distance conference call is ready," the receptionist said.

Jeff took that call and made about three more before calling it a day.

He left his office about 3:00 p.m. and headed for home, which was about fifteen miles from his office. He lived alone since his wife passed away some eighteen years ago. They had one daughter, Joyce Hanson, who lived in Dennis on the Cape with her husband and three children. His marriage was not a happy one, more a marriage of convenience. His daughter and grandchildren were probably the only people in his life that he never tried to manipulate. Jeff realized what he felt for them was probably as close to love as he would ever experience.

Before he left the office, he instructed his secretary to forward any calls from Paul Freedman to his home. I want to know as soon as Emilia is captured and on my boat he thought. He lit a cigarette at the first red light he hit. While he sat in traffic his thoughts drifted to Brad and he wondered how Brad was going to feel when he heard about Emilia. Jeff hoped he would be frantic.

It gave him immense pleasure to fantasize about Brad discovering that he was responsible for blackmailing him all these years, and in essence ruining his reputation because of the publicity surrounding his support of the APLA. He licked his lips anticipating the pleasure he would feel when Brad knew that he was responsible for taking Emilia from him. He did it once before many years ago by not giving Katherine the note Brad gave him to deliver, even though Jeff knew she was pregnant at the time. He preferred not to dwell on a few actual crimes that he viciously committed to ensure that things went his way.

Jeff was startled at the sound of the horn. He quickly looked up and noticed the light had turned green. He pulled out, took a deep drag on his cigarette and continued with his train of thought.

Jeff's philosophy was that anyone could be bought if the price was right. To make sure Katherine was not even around when Brad returned from Europe, he recruited Robert Wright, a classmate from school, to help him launch his insidious plan. The price for Robert Wright was enough money to pay off his gambling debt, which had escalated to unmanageable proportions. In fact, at the time Jeff approached him, Robert had been given one week to come up with the money. Robert accepted Jeff's proposition. He knew the syndicate did not deliver empty threats.

Jeff's car phone interrupted his thoughts. He answered and recognized his secretary's voice.

"Mr. Owensford, I'm sorry to bother you but your long distance call to California came in shortly after you left. I knew you were waiting all morning for that call but I didn't know if you wanted me to give them your home number or not."

"Perhaps you better," he said. "Since they're so hard to get hold of, I better take the call at home. Go ahead and give them my number and tell them I should be home in about thirty minutes."

Jeff's thought process continued. Katherine never knew that Jeff arranged for her to accidentally meet Robert Wright or that his motive was to see her quickly married and moved out of the area before Brad returned from Europe.

Convinced by Jeff that Brad wasn't interested in marrying her, and knowing she was pregnant, Katherine was grateful for this proposal of marriage and a new life in Plymouth. She never found out that Robert was paid to marry her.

Jeff had to laugh at the ingenious way he had taken care of everything over the years. His rise in the ranks of the APLA was definitely a contributing factor in his efforts to ruin Brad. He began to think the headaches he started to have recently might be stress related brought on by roadblocks he sometimes ran into in his crusade to destroy Brad.

Jeff rolled down his window and tossed the cigarette butt out. A few minutes later, he pulled into his garage and went into the house. He checked his answering machine first to see if he had any messages. There were none. He fixed himself a drink and went into the kitchen to find something to eat. He was anxious as he waited to hear from Paul. The last time they spoke, Paul told him that Brad reported to Chief Archer that Emilia was being followed. Jeff wasn't particularly pleased to hear that Jeremy Archer was now involved but he was determined that nothing would get in his way.

~ *NINE* ~

Emilia and Brad were in the living room playing chess when Dennis came in.

"I'm sorry," he said. "I was so engrossed in the files, I lost track of time."

"That's all right," Emilia said in a voice dripping with honey. "But don't let it happen again," she warned in an icy tone. Emilia watched Dennis struggle for an instant and then begin to laugh when he realized she was teasing him.

Emilia suggested they go into the dining room and have dinner, which was ready twenty minutes ago. She knew they were having Beef Wellington, which was one of her favorite dishes. The table was picture perfect as they sat down to eat. The Beef Wellington was done to perfection.

"Brad, your housekeeper is an excellent cook," Emilia said. "Where in the world did you ever find her?"

"She was recommended by one of my friends," Brad said. "A very good friend."

"I'm sure," Emilia said.

As they chatted while eating dinner, it was easy to forget the problem that continued to hang over their heads.

"Let's go into Sandwich after dinner and get an ice cream cone at O'Briens Ice Cream Parlor," Emilia said. "They have the best ice cream around. Then we can take a ride to the canal and see if any fancy cruise ships are coming through."

"I don't know if we should leave the house," Dennis said. "Chief Archer thinks we should stay put."

"We have the two detectives he sent over," Emilia said. "They can follow us. It's such a lovely evening; there will be a lot of people outdoors. No one would try anything in the midst of a crowd."

"She's probably right," Brad said. "We'll go and make it our number one priority to stay together and not become separated under any circumstances."

"Good," Emilia said. "If there's nothing exciting going on at the canal, we'll see if Heritage Plantation is open yet for the season. We should be back before dark." They got up from the table and she walked over and took Dennis by the arm. "If it will make you feel better, why don't you call Chief Archer and see if he'd really object to our leaving the house for a few hours."

When Dennis tried to call Chief Archer, the desk sergeant informed him that the Chief left word he was not to be disturbed unless it was an emergency. Dennis asked the sergeant to let Chief Archer know whenever he was free that they were going into Sandwich and would return before dark.

Emilia, Dennis and Brad went down through the house to the garage and all three got into Brad's car. When Brad pulled out and started down the road, he glanced in his rear view mirror and saw that Jeremy's men were right behind him. It was warm enough that Brad was able to put the top down on his convertible and they had a very enjoyable ride into Sandwich.

O'Briens was not busy when they got there. Emilia ordered a black raspberry, which was her favorite. Dennis and Brad both chose butter pecan. The next stop was the canal where they sat in the car eating their cones and watching for ships. They noticed a few couples and their children fishing from the dock.

"I guess we're not going to see any large ships coming through tonight," Emilia said. "Let's drive over to Heritage Plantation and see if it's open." It was open and they got tickets and went in.

Heritage Plantation is beautiful Emilia thought, especially when all the flowers are in bloom. It consisted of approximately 60 acres and the management provided special buses for the handicapped. There was one particular building, which housed, among other things, the oldest working merry-go-round in the United States. At special times, it was available to ride at no extra cost. Emilia always made a point to ride it when she visited Heritage Plantation. The three of them entered the building and went into a separate room to look at the merry-go-round.

"Come on, Denny," Emilia said. "Let's ride the merry-go-round."

"Oh, I don't think so," he replied. "They always make my stomach churn."

"But this one doesn't even go that fast," Emilia said. "It's a tradition."

"I'll take a ride with you," Brad said. "You're never too old to ride a merry-go-round."

Emilia and Brad walked over and got on the merry-go-round. They were the only two on the ride since no one else but Dennis was in the room at the moment. As it started up, she waved at Dennis and looked around to see if she could see Jeremy's men. They weren't in sight but she knew they must be close at hand, probably waiting outside. They went around several times when Emilia missed Dennis.

"I wonder where Denny went?" Emilia asked Brad. "He was standing over near the door a minute ago."

"I don't know," Brad replied. "I didn't see him leave. It's funny he'd leave without saying anything."

Emilia was frightened and suggested they get off the next time it came around. She was soon aware her suggestion came too late. As it came around again to face the door, Emilia saw the two men enter and start toward the merry-go-round.

"Brad, they're coming after us," Emilia cried as a feeling of terror ran through her. "What can we do?"

"When we come around again, get ready to jump off," Brad quickly said. "I'll try to hold them off. Run as fast as you can and find someone to help. Don't look back, just keep running."

Emilia's legs were like water. She couldn't move. She was rooted to the spot. As the panic welled up, she struggled to breathe. It was as though someone took a string and tied it around her throat, making it impossible to even scream.

Emilia was frozen with fear. She could not run. Hysterically she screamed at Brad, "I can't. I can't move."

Emilia felt Brad's hand on her back. At the precise moment the two men jumped on, Brad pushed Emilia off.

"Run," he screamed at her. Her natural instinct for survival took over and she immediately started to run. "Let her go," Emilia heard Brad yell. She looked back and saw Brad go down. Emilia screamed and continued to run as fast as she could.

Emilia ran around the bend of the path leading to the building and right into Chief Archer. She continued to scream as he grabbed her and held her so she couldn't move.

"Let me go," she screamed and beat against him with her fists. She assumed it was one of the men who chased her from the building. She could feel his exceptional strength and, although she had a good deal of strength herself, she couldn't get away from him. He finally held her at arms length and shook her. She looked up in shock and recognized that it was Chief Archer who had caught her. Trembling and weak with relief, she fell into his arms and he held her for a minute until she regained her composure.

"I'm sorry I shook you," he said. "I had to get your attention. Where are Owensford and McClelland?"

"Brad is hurt!" Emilia cried. She grabbed Chief Archer's hand and they raced into the building to the room with the merry-go-round. When they entered the room, she called out Brad's name. She heard a groan and ran in that direction. Brad was struggling to get to his feet. Emilia saw that his face was bruised and he had a split lip, which was bleeding profusely. She ran up and put her arms around him. She took the handkerchief Chief Archer offered and told Brad to hold it tightly against his lip to stop the bleeding.

"Thank God, you're all right," Brad mumbled. "I tried to hold them long enough for you to get away, but I wasn't sure if you'd made it."

"If you hadn't pushed me off the merry-go-round, I wouldn't have made it," she replied. "And if Chief Archer hadn't been coming along the path at just the right moment, who knows what would have happened."

"Brad, have you seen Denny yet," Emilia asked.

"No, I haven't," he replied.

"Chief, Dennis disappeared right before Brad and I noticed the two men come into the room," Emilia said. "I'm worried. I'm sure he wouldn't have gone off without telling us. We better start looking for him."

Just as the three of them started for the door, they heard someone groaning. Emilia ran outside in time to see Dennis attempting to crawl out from behind a large bush situated at the entrance door. The back of his head was covered with matted blood and he was incoherent.

"Stay with him," Chief Archer yelled. "I'll call for an ambulance. Make him lie still. It looks like he's taken a pretty bad blow to the head."

Emilia got weak all over and felt dizzy. She grabbed the door for a second until it passed. Then she knelt down on the ground and took Dennis in her arms and put his head on her lap. She could feel the hot tears streaming down her face as she called his name. He moaned but did not speak or open his eyes.

"He'll be all right," Brad tried to assure her. "He's taken a hard knock and he may have a concussion."

"Oh, Brad, he's got to be all right," Emilia said. "I love him."

"I know," Brad said. He patted her shoulder.

Emilia noticed Chief Archer coming back with a blanket. "The ambulance is on the way. In the meantime, they said to cover him and keep him warm."

"Thank you," Emilia said.

"Yes, thank you," Brad said. "For being here when we needed you. I owe you one."

When the ambulance arrived, the paramedics checked Dennis first before putting him in the ambulance. His vital signs were stable. In fact, Dennis was beginning to come out of it already. He was visibly relieved and able to relax when he realized it was Emilia holding his hand on the way to the hospital. Brad and Chief Archer followed in the Chief's car.

When they got to the hospital, the paramedics wheeled Dennis right into the emergency room. Emilia and Brad stayed behind in the waiting room. The nurse promised an update on his condition as soon as the doctor finished his examination. Emilia anticipated an extended delay after a quick scan of the waiting room revealed a good number of worried people also waiting for news of loved ones.

Brad asked Emilia if she would like a cup of coffee and he went to the gift shop. He was back in about ten minutes with their coffee. As she drank the hot coffee, Emilia decided Brad didn't look too good himself. His jaw was beginning to turn black and blue and his lip was swollen and still bleeding a little. Emilia tried to convince Brad to get checked. After all, he was sixty-five and not exactly in shape for the wrestling match he just went through.

"I think you ought to get your lip looked at," she said. "It looks as though it might require a few stitches. It will heal a lot better if you have it taken care of now. You might as well have it examined since we have to wait to hear about Denny anyway."

"I'm fine," Brad said. "A good night's sleep and I'll be as good as new."

"It will make me feel better," Emilia said.

"All right," Brad said. "I can see you'll give me no peace until I do."

Emilia watched as he went to the desk to sign in. He came back and said the nurse would call him when it was his turn. Emilia heard them call his name about twenty minutes later. If the emergency room was running true to form, he would probably lay in another small waiting area for at least twenty more minutes before someone saw him. Emilia settled back for a long wait. She took this quiet time to try and organize her thoughts and consider what their next step might entail.

Emilia got up and went to the ladies room about fifteen minutes later. When she returned, she walked over to the window and looked out at the parking lot. It was beginning to get dark and she realized it must be almost nine o'clock. Waiting was awfully hard and she was beginning to ache from the strenuous ordeal she'd just been through. She rubbed the back of her neck, flexed her arms and stretched. Emilia knew the physical reaction to stress did not occur until some time after the stress actually passed and was over. It had something to do with the fight or flight mechanism.

She jumped when a nurse called her name. She followed the nurse through the swinging doors and down a corridor to the second examining room on the right. As she entered, she noticed that Dennis was partly sitting in an upright position and was receiving intravenous fluid in his arm. On the other arm was a cuff to monitor his blood pressure. She smiled with relief when she saw him. The doctor was just finishing bandaging the back of his head.

Emilia went over to the bed and took his hand and gently kissed him. "How do you feel?" she asked. "You look a lot better than you did."

"I've got one terrific headache," Dennis replied. "The doctor here tells me I may have to put up with it for a couple of days, although they can give me something to ease it a little."

"Will he have to stay in the hospital," Emilia asked the doctor.

"I've suggested he stay at least overnight, but I'm afraid he doesn't want to take us up on our hospitality. The CAT scan didn't show a fracture, but there's always the possibility of a hemorrhage which might not show up immediately." He picked up the chart and checked it again. "If he does leave, he must be kept under observation for any symptoms, which might indicate complications, such as a change in the pupils of his eyes, extreme drowsiness, double vision or possibly nausea. We've closed the wound with about eight stitches and as soon as the antibiotic intravenous infusion is finished, he will be ready to go." Emilia saw Dennis smile. "I'll write a prescription for additional antibiotics which he can start taking tomorrow along with something for the headache. The stitches should be ready to come out in about a week."

"Thank you, doctor," Dennis said. "You've made me feel almost like a new man."

"I'll go out while you get dressed," Emilia said. "Maybe Brad will be finished now." Emilia noticed the surprised look on his face and realized Dennis didn't know that Brad was hurt too.

"I didn't realize Brad got hurt," Dennis said. "Is it very bad?"

"No, I don't think so," Emilia said. "His jaw is turning black and blue and he may need a few stitches in his lip."

"I'm sorry I wasn't there to help when you needed me," Dennis said. "I never even heard them creep up on me. I have no recollection of anything until I came to when you and Chief Archer found me."

"Don't worry about it now," Emilia said. "We'll fill you in on the way home. Chief Archer is coming back to pick us up. You get dressed now and I'll see you out in the waiting room."

When Emilia got back to the waiting room, Chief Archer was already there.

"How's Mr. McClelland?" he asked. "Where is Mr. Owensford?"

Emilia filled Chief Archer in on Dennis. "Brad went in to see about his lip," she continued. "He didn't want to but I insisted because it looked like it needed stitches. He probably should have a tetanus shot anyway. I thought maybe he would already be out here by the time I got back."

"I'm glad everything is OK," Chief Archer said. "I'll be glad when I have all of you back in Mr. Owensford's house where you'll be safe."

Emilia and Chief Archer waited for Brad and Dennis to come out. Brad came out first. He needed four stitches in his lip and they gave him a tetanus shot. He did not look happy and threatened to shoot anyone who made him laugh. Dennis came out a few minutes later.

"Let's get out of here," Chief Archer said. "I hate hospitals."

Emilia went in and got their prescriptions on the way home and filled Dennis in on all that happened while he was unconscious. When they arrived at the house, Brad invited Chief Archer in but he declined.

"You people need some rest," Chief Archer said. "I'll see you tomorrow. Make sure you have that security system locked in place."

"I will," Brad promised. "I can't thank you enough for all you've done for us today."

"By the way," Emilia asked. "What were you doing at Heritage Plantation? I meant to ask you before, but there was so much going on I forgot."

"I pulled my detectives off the case. I was there to see you safely home."

"Lucky for us you were," she said. "We owe you one."

~ *TEN* ~

Emilia felt exhausted so she was not surprised when Dennis excused himself to go to bed. She and Brad went into the living room. Emilia kicked off her shoes and literally plopped down on the sofa while Brad went to the bar to get a can of soda. She mentioned to Brad that the doctor wanted someone to wake Dennis during the night to make sure he woke easily and the pupils of his eyes were normal.

"How do you feel?" Emilia asked. "You've also been through quite a lot today."

"I don't feel too bad, considering," Brad replied. "You must be exhausted from the strain you've been under all day. I'll be fine if you feel like turning in too."

"No," she said. "I'd rather sit here and unwind for a while before I go to bed, otherwise I won't be able to go to sleep. There's nothing worse than tossing and turning all night long."

"Then let's just sit here and talk for a while," Brad said. "Tell me about Katherine. I knew she was ill but I didn't realize how serious it was. What was the problem if you don't mind my asking?"

"No, of course not," Emilia said. "She had rheumatic fever as a child and it left her with an enlarged heart. The symptoms can be alleviated sometimes for years with the proper medication, but it is progressive and will ultimately result in kidney failure and subsequent death. She made it through a bout with bacterial endocarditis but this left her very weakened and she finally did succumb. She lived approximately ten years from diagnosis until her death."

"She must have been sixty-three when she died," Brad said. "I am two years older." He got up and walked over to the bar to get a coaster. "Can I get you something to drink?"

"Yes, thank you," Emilia said. "Whatever you're having will be fine." Brad gave Emilia her drink and sat down.

"Do you believe she loved your father?" he asked. "Was she happy?"

"I can't really say," Emilia replied. "I always thought she was but we don't always feel the way others perceive that we do. Maybe we're too wrapped up in ourselves to care enough to take a good look. I know she was devoted to my father, but whether it was due to love or a sense of gratitude I guess we'll never know."

"Were you there at the end?" Brad asked.

Emilia could feel the tears sting her eyes as she remembered what it was like when she received the phone call. "No, I wasn't," she said. "I was in California when it happened. I was there for a ten-day training seminar. When the hospital called, Irene gave them my number. They informed me that she was pronounced dead one hour after the ambulance brought her to emergency." Emilia's voice broke and the tears she tried to hold back were now streaming down her face. She felt Brad's arm around her. "I'm sorry," he said. "This was not the right time for me to ask you this. Here, take a sip of your soda."

Emilia drank some of her drink and wiped her eyes. "I'm all right now," she said. "I think I've done more crying today that I can ever remember. Anyway, I called the funeral director from California and he handled everything for me. I was able to book an emergency flight home the next day. We had a closed casket because of all the weight loss and discoloring due to the kidney failure. I preferred that people remember her as she was before her illness. There's one thing I've always regretted. It's that I was not with her when she died."

"You shouldn't dwell on that," Brad said. "You had no way of knowing. Think of the many times you were there when she needed you. You can't go through life worrying about what might happen. You'd be so busy doing that; you wouldn't have time for anything else. That isn't living."

"Thanks," Emilia said. "For being so understanding." Brad went back over and sat down in his chair.

"I didn't know what to think when I received the pin," he said. "I found it strange there was no note of explanation. It wouldn't surprise me if one did turn up someday, one that was somehow inadvertently lost. I don't suppose you found anything as you went through her belongings?"

"No, I didn't," Emilia said. "But tucked between two pages in her favorite book of poems, I found a picture of the two of you standing on the beach. Of course, at the time I didn't know who the man was." She smiled. "I remember thinking they must have been in love. The picture looked worn as though it was taken out and looked at many times over the years."

Brad reached over and squeezed her hand. "Thank you," he said. "What you've told me is very comforting. I've often thought I was deluding myself to think that Katherine could still care for me after all these years, but perhaps she did."

"How did you feel when you found out I was your daughter?" Emilia asked. "Didn't you ever get the urge to contact me?"

"Oh, Emilia, you'll never know how much," Brad said. "But it would have put Katherine in a terrible position if Robert thought you were really his own. You were happy and already had a father you loved; I didn't want to spoil that for you. I'm sure you'd have felt nothing but bitter resentment toward me had I approached you with such news."

"I know you're right," Emilia said. "Knowing what I do now, I can only applaud your unselfish motive for deciding not to interfere."

Brad got up and walked over to the window. "I'd be lying if I said it was easy," he said. "But the joy at having you here now has grown even sweeter with the passage of time. I've been wanting to tell you how I felt since Denny and you arrived, but I didn't know how you'd react and the last thing I wanted to do was frighten you away."

Emilia grinned. "You won't get rid of me that easy," she said. "I hope you will always be proud to acknowledge me as your daughter. I know I shall feel privileged to say that you are my father." As Brad walked back to sit down, Emilia noticed the tears were now in his eyes.

"I'm so glad we stayed up and had this talk," he said. "You've made me very happy."

Emilia thought she heard something and went to the foot of the steps to listen. "I guess it was just the wind blowing," she said and returned and sat down on the sofa.

"I used to begrudge Robert the enjoyment and love you must have brought to his life over the years," Brad said. "When I heard he had died, I was sorry because I knew you loved him and were deeply hurt. What was he like?"

Emilia paused and was very thoughtful for a moment. "He was a very happy and optimistic person," she said. "He thought if he didn't acknowledge a problem existed, it would just disappear. That may sound like an admirable quality, but when the problem was something serious and remained so, even though he refused to see it, he would be utterly devastated. Fortunately, there were few adversities during the time I was growing up."

"Was he a good provider?" Brad asked. "I know he worked for a furniture manufacturer when they married."

"Yes, he was," Emilia replied. "My mother only mentioned one occasion shortly after I was born when things got a little tight and my father's family came to our rescue.

They weren't rich but they did have money. In fact, my mother sometimes felt they looked down their noses at her."

"How could anyone think they were better than Katherine?" Brad asked. "I get indignant at the thought of anyone treating Katherine that way." Emilia could actually hear the indignation in his voice.

"It all happened long ago," she said. "All those people have since passed away. My father was an only child so I don't have any relatives left on that side of the family. I know now that they wouldn't truly be my relatives anyway. On my mother's side, I have only one aunt who is in a nursing home."

"But you do have an Uncle Jeff in Chicago," Brad said. "Even though we are not on the best of terms. His daughter, Joyce, is your cousin. She lives right up the road in Dennis. She's very nice and I know you'll like her. We'll invite her over sometime soon so the two of you can meet."

"What does my Uncle Jeff look like?" Emilia asked. "Is he as good looking as you?"

Brad laughed. "Thank you for the compliment. I'm sure that's the nicest one I've had today. Yes, we do resemble each other. In fact, we've been mistaken for twins a few times over the years." Emilia saw that Brad was remembering some of the better times between them.

"How did your father die?" Brad asked. "I heard he died two years ago, but I don't recall any details."

"He was in an automobile accident," Emilia said. "The car went off the road and caught fire. He was burned beyond recognition."

"Oh, that's horrible," Brad said. "I had no idea."

"It was awfully hard on my mother," Emilia said. "Her health was not very good at the time and it was quite an ordeal for her to go through." Emilia got up and walked over to the window. Even though the moon was bright, the ocean looked dark and murky. She could hear the sounds of the waves hitting the stone barriers on the beach.

"She was lucky she had you," Brad said.

"I tried to spend as much time with her as I could," Emilia said. "Especially those last two years."

Brad got up and walked over to join her at the window. "You look like you're exhausted," Brad said. "Why don't you get to bed now? I'll show you to your room. There are four bedrooms on the second floor. My housekeeper put your things in the second one down the hall."

"Which one is Denny in?" Emilia asked. "I want to look in on him during the night."

"He's in the first one," Brad said. "I could check on him if you like."

"No, thanks," she said. "I want to do it. Anyway, you need to get a good night's sleep too. Besides, I'll probably have a hard time falling asleep. I usually do when I'm overly tired."

"I think if you open your window, the sound of the ocean will put you right to sleep," he said.

Brad showed Emilia to her room. She set her alarm for 3:00 a.m. to make sure she woke up to check on Dennis. Then she did as Brad suggested. She opened her window, got into bed and lay there listening to the sound of the ocean as she drifted off to sleep.

She left her window open all night and made sure she had a blanket on the bed. She remembered that as hot as it gets on the Cape during the day, the breeze from the ocean inevitably cools things off at night.

When her alarm went off at 3:00 a.m., she went next door to check on Dennis. She smiled as she remembered how startled he was when she woke him with a kiss. Before he had a chance to respond, she reminded him the doctor told her to check him during the night. When he looked disappointed, she laughed and told him he really wasn't in shape for a midnight rendezvous. She told him to go back to sleep. She returned to her room, got back into bed and went back to sleep as soon as her head hit the pillow.

When Emilia woke up again, she looked at the clock and saw it was only 6:30. She got up and went to the window to look out at the ocean. She saw Brad taking a walk along the shore. She decided to join him if he was still down there after she took her shower and got dressed.

After dressing, she looked out and saw him sitting on the rock barrier looking out toward the ocean. Hurriedly, she left her room, went downstairs, out the back door and headed for the barrier. She almost reached it before she saw him turn and look her way.

"Good morning," he called. "How did you sleep?"

"Better than I have for days," she replied. "How about you?"

"I woke up a couple of times," he said. "My jaw was hurting a little, but I wanted to check on Dennis before I took anything for the pain."

Emilia climbed up on the rocks to sit down and join Brad to look at the ocean. It was a beautiful morning. "What time did you check on him?" she asked. "I looked in on him around three o'clock. He was fine."

"I guess it was a little after four-thirty," Brad replied. "I had no trouble awakening him," he said. "Then I checked on him again before I came down here."

"I'm glad he's all right," Emilia said. "It's rare to develop complications, but since there is that slight possibility, being kept under observation for a few days is always a good idea. How does your jaw feel now?"

"It's a little better," he said. "I've found over the years that most things we struggle with during the night always look brighter and feel better in the morning."

"That's true," she said. "I hope Dennis feels the same way when he gets up."

"Speaking of the devil," Brad said. "Look who's coming to join us."

"Good morning," Emilia called. "How do you feel? Don't try to climb up here. We'll come down."

"Did anyone get the number of the truck that hit me?" Dennis asked when they reached him. Emilia and Brad laughed. Dennis put his hand up to the back of his head and winced with pain when he tried to laugh. "Oh, I must remember not to do that," he said. "It hurts my head. Promise me you won't say anything funny."

"Have either of you had anything to eat yet?" Brad asked.

"No, I haven't," Emilia said. "I wasn't sure what time you normally have breakfast."

"Nor have I," Dennis replied. "I may not care for any. Chewing might be almost as bad as laughing."

"I think I'll have a little more trouble than you," Brad said. "My lip is so swollen it's sure to get in my way."

"You two are certainly a couple of sad cases," Emilia said. "Want to race to the house, Denny?" she asked.

"You promised not to say anything funny," he reminded her. "I'm afraid if I were able to run at all, it would be like an old nag who was put out to pasture."

"I'm sorry," she said. "I did promise to behave. Do you want me to go up and put the coffee on?"

"Yes, I could use a cup of coffee," Dennis said.

"You go up and make the coffee," Brad said. "Dennis and I will sit here on the beach for a while. My housekeeper should be here in about fifteen minutes and then we'll have breakfast."

"Do you want breakfast on the deck?" Emilia asked as she headed for the steps.

"Yes, that would be nice," Brad said. "I usually eat out there when the weather permits."

"I'll let you know when it's ready," Emilia called back as she ran up the steps onto the deck. She looked back and saw Brad and Dennis walk over and sit down close to the shoreline.

A few minutes later, Emilia called to them that the coffee would be ready in about five minutes.

"We'll be right up," Dennis called up to her. "It will probably take me five minutes to get up to the house."

When they got to the house, Dennis sat down at the table on the deck and Brad headed into the house. Emilia was just bringing out the coffeepot and cups. "It's ready," she said.

"I'll be right back," Brad said. "I have to make a phone call."

Emilia was pouring Dennis a cup of coffee when Brad returned.

"That was fast," she said.

"I called Chief Archer but he wasn't in yet," Brad replied. He got himself a cup and Emilia poured his coffee. "I left word for him to call."

"Our breakfast will be ready soon," Emilia said. She walked over to the railing to watch the seagulls who were circling what appeared to be a school of fish not too far out from shore. She heard Brad's housekeeper tell him he had a call from Chief Archer.

Emilia and Dennis were almost finished eating when Brad returned. He told them Chief Archer was coming to the house around noon with two applicants for Emilia to interview as bodyguards. Emilia listened as Brad told them Chief Archer considered these two to have the best qualifications, but the final decision would be hers. Emilia and Dennis had another cup of coffee and kept Brad company while he ate his breakfast.

After breakfast, Emilia left Brad and Dennis to talk while she went inside to call Irene. She wanted to be assured everything was under control. With the exception of a call from Chuck Collins, most of the other calls were for brochures, explaining the smoking cessation program, which Irene routinely sent out.

"Did Chuck say what he wanted?" Emilia asked.

"Yes, he wanted to know if you would be available for a meeting at the high school on Friday afternoon. Right now there is a tentative time of 2:30 p.m."

"Did he say what the meeting is about?" Emilia asked.

"It concerns that confrontation between the teachers and the APLA." Emilia remembered him telling them about it at the restaurant Monday night.

"Yes, I remember," Emilia said. "He thought at the time it might spell trouble. I guess he was right. Call and let him know I'll plan on attending. I should be in the office all day tomorrow."

Emilia briefly told Irene what happened at Heritage Plantation, promising more details when she saw her, and let her know two bodyguards would in all likelihood accompany her to the office.

When Emilia finished talking to Irene, she joined Brad and Dennis outside. Dennis was reading the newspaper when Brad asked her if she'd like to go for a walk on the beach. Emilia asked Dennis to join them but he declined. After Emilia and Brad had gone down to the beach, the housekeeper told Dennis he had a phone call but they gave no name.

- ELEVEN -

Dennis wondered who would be calling him this early in the morning as he went into the living room to get the phone. Still a bit wobbly from the blow to his head, he sat down on a chair before picking up the phone.

"Hello, this is Dennis McClelland," he said.

"Mr. McClelland, my name is Steve Lawson. I'm an agent with the FBI. Are you alone? Can you talk freely?"

"Yes, what's this about?" Dennis asked.

"It concerns Brad Owensford and his reputed involvement with the APLA. The FBI is actively working on this case and has been for the past two years. We are aware that Brad Owensford has been an unwilling supporter of this organization for many years. Agent Ed Bradley, my partner, and I wanted to know if you would be willing to assist us on this case. With your help, we might be able to get the matter resolved in a more timely fashion."

"Absolutely," Dennis said. "I'll do whatever I can." Dennis then listened as Agent Lawson continued.

"Before we accept your help, I feel it only fair to mention one drawback which could present a problem for you someday. If, for any reason whatever, anyone were to ever make an inquiry about your participation in this case, the FBI would emphatically deny your involvement or ever hearing your name. Your experience as a private detective should immediately bring to mind how this could prove to be embarrassing as well as dangerous. If you would like to withdraw your offer of help, I will understand and think none the less of you."

"I understand perfectly what you're telling me," Dennis said. "My offer still holds."

"I was hoping that would be your answer," Agent Lawson said. "But we don't want to discuss this on the telephone. Could you suggest a place where we might meet in private and not be interrupted?"

"Yes, I can," Dennis replied. "I have an office in Sandwich. We won't be disturbed there. What time would be best for you?"

"Whenever you say," Agent Lawson replied. "We're free right now if you are."

Dennis gave them directions to his office and they agreed to meet in twenty minutes. Before leaving, he left word for Emilia that he was going into town for a few hours and should be back around noon.

Dennis noticed it was 10:00 a.m. when Agents Lawson and Bradley arrived at his office.

"Sorry, we're a little late," Agent Lawson said. "Seems to be an awful lot of traffic this morning."

"Traffic is usually heavier on Wednesday," Dennis said. "We're not sure why, maybe it's a good grocery shopping day. Please sit down. There's coffee on the table there. Help yourself."

"Thanks," Agent Lawson said. He and Agent Bradley both got a cup of coffee before they sat down. "We heard what happened at Heritage Plantation last night. Could you give us an update on that?"

"There's really not a whole lot to tell," Dennis said. He put his coffee down and leaned back in his chair. "Mr. Owensford, Miss Wright and I were in the building which houses the old merry-go-round. I was hit on the head from behind and was unconscious through the rest of it. I understand there were two men. Mr. Owensford was able to hold them back while Miss Wright got away. If Chief Archer's arrival had been delayed by a few minutes, they might have succeeded in the abduction. As it was, Mr. Owensford and I both needed a few stitches and Miss Wright was pretty badly shaken up. We are very much aware it could have been much worse. We plan on hiring two bodyguards this afternoon for Miss Wright. Chief Archer suggested the bodyguards and I concurred."

"We're going to give you some facts about this case," Agent Lawson said. Dennis was not surprised when he insisted they be held in strict confidence. "I'm sure you will find some of them rather startling, which is primarily the reason for secrecy."

"I understand," Dennis said. "It will be kept confidential." He got up and went to the table for some hot coffee.

Agent Lawson took a notebook from his inside coat pocket. "We'll begin with Brad Owensford's brother, Jeff. We believe that Jeff Owensford initiated the extortion threat against Brad Owensford some forty years ago. Jeff Owensford is also an inactive corporate officer with the APLA and has been all these years."

"I can't believe what you're saying," Dennis interrupted. "How could Brad's own brother do such a thing to him. What possible reason could he have to put Brad through such hell all these years? How do you know this is true?"

"We have an informer who has successfully become affiliated with the organization," Agent Bradley said. Dennis then listened as he told him, among other things, how their informer profiled Jeff Owensford as appearing to suffer from unrealistic delusions of grandeur. He once heard him tell an associate that their organization, with Jeff in charge, would one day rule the country.

"Brad will be devastated when he learns of his brother's treachery," Dennis said. He wondered if Brad knew his brother was thought to have a delusional disorder. He didn't recall if Brad ever mentioned it.

"I assume you already know that the APLA has credited Brad Owensford as being their largest financial supporter," Agent Lawson said. "Not only has Jeff

Owensford seen to it that Brad Owensford's money has gone to this anti-American organization, but has made sure that the whole world knew in order to ruin his reputation."

"They have been extremely successful," Dennis said. "I hope someday the whole world will also be privy to the truth. Maybe the activities of the APLA will be cut back drastically when they lose the support of Brad Owensford's money. We might even hope the loss will be enough to put them under."

"That's what we're working toward," Agent Lawson said. "We're beginning to see a light at the end of the tunnel. Jeff Owensford is getting careless and we're just waiting for him to slip."

"Have you ever heard of Paul Freedman?" Agent Bradley asked.

"No, I haven't," Dennis replied. "Who is he?"

"We believe he may be Katherine Wright's brother, Andrew O'Brien, who disappeared years ago. Our sources tell us Jeff Owensford found him wandering the streets of Chicago, close to death from a severe blow to the head. He took him to the hospital where he regained his health but was left with amnesia. He began working for Jeff Owensford in no specific capacity, but was assigned various tasks at Jeff Owensford's discretion."

"You weren't exaggerating when you promised I would hear some startling facts!" Dennis exclaimed. He got up and went to look out the window.

"We don't believe Paul Freedman is particularly fond of his work," Agent Lawson said. "But he has this sense of obligation which keeps him there. If we are right in our assumption of his identity, then it's possible Jeff Owensford was responsible for his beating. It would also explain why he has kept Paul with him all these years. The hospital records indicated there was a slight chance his memory might return someday."

"Is there any way to be sure if that's who he is?" Dennis asked.

"Maybe, if we could get our hands on an old photograph of Andrew," Agent Lawson replied. "He will definitely be in danger if his memory suddenly returns."

"I can understand why," Dennis said. He got himself another cup of coffee and sat down at his desk. "He would probably be signing his own death warrant. Maybe I could get one for you on some pretext or other."

"That would be great," Agent Bradley said. "Do you have any questions before we wrap this up?"

"There is something I was wondering about, Dennis said. "Did Jeff Owensford have anything to do with Katherine Wright leaving the Cape before Brad Owensford returned from Europe?"

"We're sure he did," Agent Lawson said. "He introduced her to Robert Wright, who was a classmate of his in college, and they were married within the month. We believe that Robert Wright promised to marry Katherine in exchange for Jeff Owensford's payment of his gambling debts. His addiction to gambling was what enabled Jeff Owensford to manipulate him."

"Do you think Robert Wright knew Brad Owensford was Emilia's father?" Dennis asked. "Or don't you know?"

"We're not sure if he knew or not," Agent Bradley replied. "He had to know he was not her father. To his credit, all reports indicate he was a loving father to Emilia, never giving her any reason to suspect he was not her biological father."

Dennis leaned forward and rubbed the back of his neck. His medication was wearing off and his head was beginning to throb. "It's going to take me a while to digest all that you've just told me," Dennis said. "This bump on my head isn't helping either. I'll be able to concentrate a little better after I take a pain pill."

"You take your time," Agent Lawson said. "Agent Bradley and I have a couple of things to take care of this afternoon. We'll give you a call later and discuss what our first priority will be and how you'll be able to help us."

"You can count on me," Dennis said as he walked them to the door. "I'll be leaving myself in a few minutes."

Dennis looked through his mail and checked his answering machine before he locked the door and headed back to Brad's house.

- *TWELVE* -

Emilia looked up from her almost finished lunch and saw Chief Archer and two men walking toward them. They must be the bodyguards she thought. She and Brad were promptly introduced to Bill Stewart and Howard McMillen.

"Please sit down and join us," Emilia said. "Would you like some coffee or iced tea?"

"No, thank you," Bill Steward said as he sat down. "They served a light lunch on the plane just before we landed."

"Where is Mr. McClelland?" Chief Archer asked. "I thought he was staying here with you."

"He is," Brad said. "He went to his office. He should be back any minute."

Emilia listened as Brad discussed their assignment and both men contributed input, which clearly demonstrated their qualifications for the job. She felt that Brad was obviously satisfied with Chief Archer's selection. Emilia told Brad that she, too, found them very qualified to provide her protection.

Emilia went over her schedule with Bill and Howard, as they requested she call them, as Brad saw Chief Archer to the door. She was asking them if they had any questions when Brad returned. Dennis was with him and Emilia noticed he didn't look too well.

"You better sit down and have something to eat," she said. "You should have waited a couple of days before you went to your office. You look exhausted. Does your head hurt?" She poured him a glass of iced tea.

"Yes, it started to get worse right before I left the office," Dennis said. "Would you mind getting my pills for me. They're on my nightstand."

"I'll get them," Brad said. "I'm going upstairs for some paperwork I forgot."

Emilia was surprised at how quickly Brad returned. She sensed he was also concerned by the way Dennis looked. Emilia got him a glass of water and he took his pill. "Now, you eat something," she ordered.

Emilia heard Brad ask Bill and Howard if they would like to see the grounds.

"Yes, I think that would be a good idea," Bill replied. "Becoming familiar with the area is always an advantage, especially if Miss Wright is going to be a frequent visitor here."

"Yes, she will," Brad said as they walked down the steps.

Emilia listened to their conversation as they left the deck and she liked what she heard very much. She looked at Dennis and saw that the color was coming back to his face as he ate his lunch.

"You look better," she said. "I think you're going to live."

"I feel better," Dennis said. "How do you like the bodyguards Chief Archer brought?"

"I think they will work out just fine," she said. "Of course, I'd much rather have you." She stood behind his chair and massaged his shoulders and neck. She could feel the tight muscles in his shoulders begin to relax as she kneaded them with her hands.

"Oh, that feels so good," Dennis said. "Don't stop."

"You're going to miss me when I'm gone tomorrow," she said. Dennis grabbed her hands and pulled her onto his lap. He put his arms around her. "I'm going too."

"Oh, no, you're not," Emilia said. "You're staying here to rest at least another day. I don't want you getting any complications from that head injury." She gave him a kiss and got up when she heard Brad returning with Bill and Howard.

Emilia walked over to the railing when they came up on the deck.

"Is there anything else you need from me?" Emilia asked.

"No, that just about covers it," Bill said. "Please don't be concerned if we're not always visible. Just be assured that we're here."

"That's very comforting to know," Emilia said. "Thanks a lot. By the way, I'll be leaving for Plymouth around 7:45 tomorrow morning to go to my office."

"All right," Howard said. "We'll be ready."

Emilia watched as Bill and Howard left the deck and walked around the side of the house and out of sight. "Let's go into the living room and relax for a while," she suggested to Dennis and Brad.

They had just gotten comfortable, Emilia and Dennis on the sofa and Brad in the easy chair, when Emilia heard the doorbell ring. She watched Brad pull himself out of the chair to see who it was. She heard him say, "Come in Joyce. It's good to see you." Emilia remembered Brad mentioned she had a cousin who lived in Dennis, his brother Jeff's daughter. Emilia decided as they came into the room that Joyce Hanson was very nice looking.

"Emilia, this is Joyce Hanson, my niece." Brad said. "I think you already know Dennis. Come over here and sit down."

"Yes, I do," she said. "How are you Dennis? It's been a long time. I'm glad to meet you Emilia."

"I'm fine," Dennis said. "Emilia is taking good care of me." Emilia felt Dennis put his arm around her. Emilia knew Joyce noticed it and was wondering about her.

"Is Emilia a friend of yours?" Joyce asked Dennis.

"Not exactly," Brad replied before Dennis had a chance to answer. "I'm certain this will come as a surprise, but Emilia is my daughter."

"I never knew you were married, let alone had a daughter," Joyce said. "Was this some family secret? I'm sure my father never mentioned it."

Emilia listened as Brad filled Joyce in on their background. She watched Joyce closely and tried to read her reaction by studying her face as Brad related the details, as he knew them. Emilia was glad to see that the only thing Joyce revealed was surprise. She waited for Joyce to respond.

"Did you know Uncle Brad was your father?" Joyce asked Emilia.

"No, I didn't," Emilia said. "I grew up believing Robert Wright was my father. I only found out about Brad a few days ago. In fact, I only met Dennis a few days ago."

"It sounds like a fairy tale come true," Joyce said. "I'm very happy for you. I hope you and I will be good friends as well as cousins." Emilia smiled and noticed that Brad looked quite pleased.

"I hoped you would feel that way," Brad said. "But you don't look too happy. Is something the matter? Is that why you stopped to see me? I'll get us some iced tea while you tell me about it." Emilia saw that Brad was limping when he walked over to the bar to get their drinks. She wondered if he hurt his leg during the scuffle last night.

"I never could hide anything from you," Joyce said. "It's dad." Emilia sensed the worry in Joyce's voice as she described her father's behavior. "He's becoming very withdrawn and hostile. At first I thought it was my imagination, but Mike and the kids have seen it too. When he was here the last time, I tried to discuss it and even suggested he have a complete checkup. He became quite indignant and practically told me to mind my own business. I'm truly worried, especially since he lives alone and so far away in Chicago. He doesn't even call anymore, and when I call him he is very cold and distant with me."

"I'm sorry to hear that," Brad said.

"Isn't there anything you can do?" Emilia asked. "You're so good with people."

"I'd be glad to talk to him," Brad said. "But Joyce knows how he feels about me. I've never understood the reasoning behind it, and although I've tried many times over the years to rectify the situation, he continues to reject my attempts at reconciliation."

"I know that," Joyce said. "If he's like that with us, I'm sure he would be much worse with you."

"He may listen this time if he's sick," Emilia said. "Sometimes when you're sick, you have to give up your independence and accept a little help when it's offered."

"I really shouldn't burden you with my problems," Joyce said. "You've got enough of your own right now. But thanks for listening." Emilia wished there was something she could do to help Joyce. She sounded so down in the dumps.

"We'll always be here to listen," Brad said. "I just wish there was something I could do."

Emilia felt Dennis looking back and forth at her and Joyce.

"Have you noticed their eyes, Brad?" Dennis asked. "You Owensfords must all be endowed with them."

"To tell you the truth, I hadn't noticed," Brad said. "I do now that you've called my attention to it. I guess it is an Owensford characteristic. I think Jeff's eyes are the same, aren't they, Joyce?" Emilia waited to hear what Joyce would say. She was a little curious about Jeff Owensford.

"Yes, they most certainly are," Joyce replied. "People used to say we could lay someone out in flowers with just a look."

"I've never heard that expression," Emilia said. "Although my friends invariably know when I'm angry just by looking at my eyes. They say it's a fearful thing to behold." Emilia noticed how congenial and at ease everyone was and it made her happy.

"How about the four of us going out to dinner?" Brad asked. "It will be my treat."

"I'd love to," Joyce said. "I'll have to phone home first."

"That would be nice," Dennis said. "Emilia needs a little recreation."

Emilia laughed. "Speak for yourself," she said. "Are you sure you're up to it?"

"I'm feeling better every minute," Dennis replied.

"I was going to inquire about the bruise you have, Uncle Brad," Joyce said. "I didn't want to pry. Now that I see Dennis is wounded too, I'm wondering what the other guy must look like."

With that, they all began laughing. Then Emilia filled Joyce in on what had taken place last evening and up to the hiring of the two bodyguards today.

"I was wondering who the two men were standing off to the side of the house when I came in," Joyce said. "I completely forgot to ask you after we began to visit."

"They will also be following us when we leave for dinner," Emilia said. "Perhaps I'll let them know where we're going while Joyce makes her phone call."

"Where will we be going?" Dennis asked. Emilia waited to hear where Brad wanted to go so she could let Bill and Howard know.

"There's a new seafood restaurant in Hyannis that opened last week," Brad responded. "I hear the lobster is out of this world."

While Emilia went to talk to Bill and Howard, Joyce called home and Brad went to change his clothes. Emilia, Joyce and Dennis were ready and waiting for Brad at the front door when he came down the steps. "Is everyone ready?" he asked.

"We're waiting for you," Emilia said.

"Then let's get going and beat the crowd," Brad said. Emilia watched as he locked the front door and carefully activated the alarm system.

Emilia couldn't remember having a better time. The restaurant was excellent and matched the company. The night was warm and on the way home, Brad put the top down on his convertible. She looked back a few times after they dropped Joyce off and observed that Bill and Howard were close behind them. Just knowing they were there instilled a sense of peace she hadn't felt in days. It was very reassuring to her that she would be in their company when she returned to Plymouth tomorrow.

As though reading her thoughts, Dennis asked, "What time will you be leaving in the morning?"

"I'd like to be at the office by 8:30," she replied. "So I'll plan on leaving about 7:45 which will allow a little extra time in case the traffic is heavy."

"I can be ready by then," Dennis said. "Make sure I'm up by 7:00."

"I really don't think you should go," she said. "You ought to stay here and recuperate for at least another day. Don't you agree, Brad?"

"Yes, I do," Brad said. "You don't want to rush it, Denny. If the doctor had his way, you would still be in the hospital under observation. There's no reason you have to go. Emilia will be fine; she's got Bill and Howard looking after her and I've got complete confidence in them." Emilia was glad of Brad's support.

"If that's what you want," Dennis said. "I can see it's two against one. I wish you would come back after work."

"I can't do that," she said. "I've got to get back to my apartment. Aside from my clothes, there are other things that require my attention. There's absolutely no reason for you to be concerned. You know I live in a secured apartment complex and Bill and Howard will be with me."

"OK, I'm convinced," Dennis said as Brad pulled into the driveway. Emilia and Dennis got out and waited until Brad put the car in the garage and joined them at the front door.

"I think I'll take a quick walk on the beach before it gets dark," Emilia said. "You two want to come along?"

"You and Denny go," Brad replied. "I think I'll go inside and watch the news."

A few minutes later, Emilia and Dennis walked up the beach hand in hand. They walked along in silence, each deep in thought. Then Dennis asked, "When are you and I getting married?"

Emilia laughed. "Is this a proposal?" she asked. "I thought the fellow was supposed to get down on one knee, take his beloved by the hand, profess his deep and undying love and ask for her hand in marriage. That's the way they do it in the movies."

Dennis stopped walking and turned toward her and looked into her eyes. "I'll do it anyway you want, as long as the answer is yes," he said. "I feel as though I've known you all my life, and I want to spend the rest of my days with you."

"You know the answer is yes," she said.

"Then let's make it soon," he said. "Let's not waste another precious minute."

With that, he took her in his arms, held her tightly to him and kissed her long and hard. She knew his passion as she felt his heart beating against her, and when he released her, she was breathless with a desire that matched his own. If she'd had any doubt before, it vanished when Dennis held her in his arms.

Later, as they walked toward the house, they decided to tell Brad they were engaged. They found him sitting on the deck reading his newspaper.

"Brad, we have something to tell you," she said. "Denny and I are engaged." Brad got up out of his chair and Emilia, as well as Dennis, received a big bear hug.

"I couldn't be happier," he said. "But I must admit I'm not surprised. I saw it coming. Have you set a date?"

"We haven't gotten that far," Emilia said. "You'll be the first to know when we do. I think I'll turn in now. I want to get up at 6:00 a.m. and take a walk on the beach before breakfast. See the two of you in the morning."

"Good night," Brad said. "Sweet dreams."

Emilia kissed Dennis good night and then went inside to get ready for tomorrow.

~ *THIRTEEN* ~

Jeff Owensford had just dozed off again when he heard the phone ringing. Now what joker would be calling this early in the morning he wondered? He reached over to the nightstand and picked up the phone. "Hello," he snapped.

"Jeff, this is Paul. I know it's early but I figured you might want to know what happened last night."

"Did they get her?" Jeff asked. He made no effort to conceal the excitement in his voice. "Is she on the boat?"

"No, they didn't," Paul said. "There was quite a fiasco on the Cape last night. Our men really bungled things. They tried to grab Emilia but failed in the attempt."

"Did they get caught?" Jeff asked. He felt on the nightstand for his cigarettes and lit one.

"No, they were lucky this time," Paul replied. "They got away but they may have been seen by Chief Archer's men who were assigned to follow Emilia."

"I'm afraid their usefulness to us may be over," Jeff said. "Has there been anything on the air about it?"

"I don't think so," Paul said.

"Where did all this take place?" Jeff asked.

"At Heritage Plantation," Paul replied. "They did come close to pulling it off. If Chief Archer hadn't come on the scene when he did, I think they would have had her. One of our people got a little rough. He gave Dennis McClelland quite a blow to the head. He was taken to the hospital and required several stitches, but they did release him."

"What about Brad?" Jeff asked. "Was he also hurt?" Jeff's tone did not indicate concern, just curiosity.

"I understand Brad Owensford was knocked down and has a bruised jaw and needed a couple of stitches in his lip. Do you have an alternate plan?" Paul asked.

"Not really, but I'm sure it will have to be done on the Cape," Jeff replied. "Let's wait and see what their next move will be. Where are our people now?"

"They're parked at the canal waiting for further instructions," Paul said.

"Tell them to come back to Chicago," Jeff said. "I want them to leave right now. When they get here, you can send them out to Denver to join that small activist group we're sponsoring. They can join as concerned citizens. Make them responsible for daily reports on activities going on within the group and, in particular, supplying names of individuals they feel might be naïve enough to accept our philosophy."

"How long should they plan on staying there?" Paul asked.

"At least until we're sure they won't be recognized if we send them back to the Cape," Jeff said. "This may be one you'll have to handle yourself." Jeff knew Paul would never be capable of doing the job, but he derived great pleasure out of making Paul sweat. Even the suggestion was enough to send Paul into a tizzy.

"I really don't think I could do that," Paul said in a shaky voice. "Is there anything else?"

"I want you to cover a meeting for me on Friday afternoon," Jeff said. "It's being held at the Plymouth High School. If you fly out early Friday morning, you should have no trouble being there by two-thirty."

"All right," Paul said. "Any special instructions or do you just want me to take notes as an interested citizen?"

"That's all I need right now," Jeff said. "For your information, this meeting was called by the Superintendent of the Plymouth School District in an effort to stop our introduction of books into their school libraries."

"Are these specific books, or books in general?" Paul asked.

"They are the series of children's books we had published last year to introduce homosexuality as a choice of life style," he said. "We figure it will end up in court and if we are successful and win our case, then a precedent will be set which will enable us to contaminate the entire United States Public School System."

"I honestly can't condone what you're planning," Paul said. "Surely you're not purposely planning the destruction of this country through its children."

Jeff laughed. "That's only one way. We have a long agenda in our files." Jeff knew he had shocked Paul with the openness of his remarks. He made no effort to mask his evil intent and he let Paul know he expected him to remain loyal as always. Jeff also made it clear he was not interested in Paul's opinion, only his cooperation.

"I'll call now and make reservations," Paul said. "When I get back, I want to talk to you about my retirement. Janet and I are ready. We plan on selling our home and moving to a small retirement community in Ohio."

"We'll talk about it when you come back," Jeff said. "In fact, we'll discuss it when you bring the report to my office. See you then."

When Jeff hung up, he realized Paul's usefulness was over. He hadn't decided yet if he would have him eliminated. He wondered if it were still possible for him to regain his memory after all these years. Aside from that, Jeff realized Paul knew entirely too much to allow him to just pick up and leave. No immediate decision had to be made; it would be a simple matter to take care of when the time came.

Right now, he felt another of those terrible headaches coming on. He would have to lie down until the throbbing subsided. Maybe Joyce was right about seeing a doctor. He could at least give him something for this excruciating pain.

The aspirin he bought at the drug store last night brought him no relief at all. But then as he pressed his hands to his temples, he suddenly remembered he could no longer trust Joyce since he knew she was plotting to get her hands on his money. The voices he heard had told him this. He wasn't fooled by her feigned concern for his health. He could tell by her eyes that she secretly hated him and wished him dead. They were all jealous of his great success and were conspiring against him, especially his brother, Brad. But they could do nothing to him because he could feel a power within him, which was making him invincible. He would soon take over the whole country.

Jeff began to laugh uncontrollably as he fell onto the bed in unconscious oblivion.

The ringing of the phone a few hours later brought him back to a pain free reality. He got up and crossed the room to pick up the phone.

"Hello," he answered in a voice barely audible.

"Jeff, this is Brad. Joyce told me earlier today that you're not feeling well and she's very concerned. Is there anything I can do?"

"I'm all right," Jeff said. "I told her it's probably some bug or other. I wish she'd mind her own business and stop worrying about me. The same goes for you."

"If that's what you want," Brad said. "I just wanted to help. I wish you'd consider going to the doctor and getting a checkup as Joyce suggested."

"When I need a checkup, I'll get one," Jeff shouted. "Now get off my back."

With that, he hung up the phone. He looked at the clock and saw that he'd been out for a couple of hours. He was concerned for he realized that each time it happened, he seemed to be unconscious for a longer period of time. He would call this afternoon and make an appointment. He had too many irons in the fire to risk getting sick and becoming incapacitated. One of those irons was Emilia Wright.

~ FOURTEEN ~

Emilia awoke the next morning at 6:00 a.m. and got right up so she'd have time for a walk on the beach before breakfast. In a way, she hated the thought of going back to Plymouth. It was hard to believe she had only been here two days, so much had happened. She wished the problem they had to resolve would suddenly disappear. Now that she was looking forward to her future with Dennis, she just wanted to put it behind her and get on with her life.

She got dressed and went for her walk. When she got back to the house, Brad and Dennis were just sitting down at the table in the dining room. Emilia expected them to be eating indoors because the sky had darkened and it was beginning to drizzle.

"It looks like I got here just in time," she said. "That sea air sure gives me an appetite." Emilia sat down and joined them as Brad poured her coffee.

"I should be able to put my affairs in order in a few days," she said. "I only have one appointment tomorrow. It's with Chuck Collins, the head of the Plymouth School District. Some trouble with the APLA. He's asked that I attend a meeting at the school tomorrow afternoon and I told Irene to tell him I'd be there. Maybe I'll be able to get back late tomorrow night or early Saturday morning. You don't know how much I'll miss the two of you." She noticed how quiet Brad and Dennis were through breakfast.

After they finished eating, Emilia went upstairs to change clothes and get her bag. When she came back down, she saw Dennis and Brad waiting at the front door to say good-bye. She knew by their faces that they were going to miss her.

"I'll call you later tonight," she said and gave Brad a hug.

"You take care," Dennis said as he kissed her goodbye.

She blew them a kiss as she stepped into the back of the car. Bill was driving and Howard sat opposite him on the passenger side of the front seat. Emilia wished she were returning rather than leaving. For one brief moment, she shivered with apprehension about the next few days.

Emilia was surprised at how light the traffic was on their drive to Plymouth. She walked into her outer office accompanied by Bill Stewart and Howard McMillen at 8:20. She looked for Irene and saw her filing in the file cabinet along the back wall.

"Hi, Irene," Emilia said. "Anything new this morning?"

"No, everything is quiet for a change," Irene replied. "Two of our moderators were in to pick up literature to pass out at their meetings tonight and that's about all. The only appointment I made for you is with Chuck Collins. He'll be here around two o'clock this afternoon."

"Irene, this is Bill Stewart and Howard McMillen," Emilia said. "They are the two bodyguards I told you about, and they will be spending most of their time in the reception area with you as long as I am in the office."

"Fine," Irene said. "There's coffee over there on the corner table next to the magazine rack. Please feel free to help yourself. And those two chairs over on the side wall are the most comfortable, especially if you're going to be spending all day here."

"Thanks, Irene," Howard said. "Don't pay us any mind. Pretend we're not even here." Emilia went into her office and left them to get acquainted.

As she sat down at her desk, she noticed the pin was still lying where she left it. It brought back a flood of memories and she realized with profound sadness how much she missed her mother. She knew her mother had always loved Brad Owensford even though she married Robert Wright. She suddenly remembered she promised to fill Irene in on what happened Tuesday night.

Emilia hit the intercom button and said, "Irene, would you please come in?"

"Be right there," Irene replied. "Should I bring a notepad?"

"No, not right now," Emilia said.

She watched as Irene came in and sat down in the chair opposite her desk. "I promised to fill you in on what happened Tuesday night," she said.

"That's right," Irene said. "You did."

Emilia told Irene about the entire incident. She enjoyed watching the various expressions on Irene's face as she gave her a blow by blow description of the actual abduction attempt. By the time she finished her story, Emilia was sure Irene understood why she hired the bodyguards.

Emilia and Irene left for lunch about noon and returned at one o'clock. Bill Stewart accompanied them, and Howard went to lunch when Bill returned. Emilia knew that Bill and Howard had electronic contact with each other at all times even though they might be physically separated for short periods of time.

Chuck Collins arrived at two o'clock and, after getting a nod of confirmation from Irene to the two men seated to her right, was told to go right in.

Emilia looked up as Chuck opened the door and came in. She was on the phone and motioned for him to sit down, holding a finger up that she would just be a minute. He sat down and looked around until she finished her call and hung up.

"Hello," he said. "It's none of my business, but what's with the two gentlemen sitting in your outer office? It looked as though Irene gave them the nod that I had passed inspection and was permitted to see you. Or is my imagination playing tricks?"

Emilia laughed. "No, your imagination is intact," she said. "They are my two bodyguards."

"You are going to tell me why you require bodyguards, aren't you?" he asked.

"Yes, I am," she said. Emilia told Chuck Collins everything that happened to her since she saw him in the restaurant Monday evening.

"No one could accuse you of leading a dull life the last two days," Chuck said. "It seems to be equally divided between good and evil. I can't wait to meet this Dennis McClelland who has swept you off your feet."

"I'll make sure you meet him very soon," she said. "Now what can I do for you today?"

"Nothing today," Chuck said. "I wanted to fill you in on the nature of the meeting tomorrow afternoon. You already know it involves the APLA."

"Yes, you mentioned there might be a bit of trouble when we met you at the restaurant Monday night. You know you can count on me to help in any way I can. Suppose you fill me in on the details."

"It's about a series of children's books they are insisting we make a part of our school library. They have intimated that if we do not agree, a suit will be entered against us in Federal Court. The School Board called the meeting to inform the parents of the situation and get their reaction. We are prepared to fight this in court if the parents feel as strongly as we do about the issue."

"What kind of books are they?" Emilia asked. "I'm sorry, would you like a cup of coffee?"

"If you're having one," he replied.

"What would you like in it?" she asked.

"Just black," Chuck replied.

Emilia buzzed Irene and asked her to bring in two cups of coffee.

"You were going to tell me about the books," Emilia said.

"Yes," Chuck said. "They are books promoting homosexuality as a choice of life style. You and I both agree, there is nothing normal about homosexuality and it shouldn't be flaunted as something desirable. Aside from not being physically normal, it is morally unacceptable in most religious denominations. But it is the sin, or the sexual preference itself if you are looking at it from a secular viewpoint, that is not acceptable. We would feel the same about children's books which gave guidelines or choices to steal, cheat, lie or any other unacceptable behavior."

"You're absolutely right," Emilia was saying as Irene came in with the coffee. She continued as Irene quietly put their coffee on the desk and left. "You are not refusing these books because of discrimination against gays themselves. They will have a hard time proving otherwise. Remember, when they were seeking minority status in their claims of discrimination in the workplace? They were practically laughed out of court because, almost without exception, their positions and salaries were at the top of the pay scale."

"I don't recall hearing about that," Chuck said. "It probably didn't generate much interest because it was one they lost." Emilia laughed.

"I'm glad you'll be at the meeting," Chuck said. He took another drink of coffee. "I might call on you to be an active participant. I'm hoping we can persuade them to withdraw their request by a public show of support."

"We'll give it our best shot," she said. "They don't normally go away since they have unlimited funds to pay their court fees whether they win or lose. But that may change someday soon."

"Thanks again," Chuck said as he stood up to leave. "I'll see you tomorrow."

Emilia got up and walked Chuck to the door before she sat down at her desk to finish the project she was working on before he arrived. She left the office around four o'clock with Bill and Howard, leaving Irene to switch on the voice mail and lock up.

As soon as Emilia got home, she put through a call to Brad and Dennis. It was Brad who answered the phone. She could tell by the sound of his voice that he was happy to hear from her.

"How are you two getting along without me today?" she asked.

"We're all right, but we miss you," he said. "Anything new?"

"No, not really," she said. "I think I've got everything under control at the office. How's Denny?"

"He's fine. Of course, he's been moping around since you left. I've been showing him some of my old picture albums. He wanted to see pictures of Katherine's family, too, but I don't have any except those of Katherine. I guess he heard the phone ring. He's here now patiently waiting for me to shut up so he can talk to you, so I guess we better put him out of his misery. Give me a call tomorrow," Brad said and handed the phone to Dennis.

"Hi there," Dennis said. "I missed you today."

"I missed you," Emilia said. "How's your head?" She listened as Dennis told her he couldn't wait to get his stitches out and felt like a dirt ball because he couldn't wash his hair when he showered. "When are you supposed to go back?" she asked.

"I'm pretty sure the doctor said in a week," Dennis replied.

"I understand you've been looking at picture albums all day," she said. "Brad said you wanted to see pictures of my family but he only has pictures of my mother. I'll have to find some of my pictures and bring them back with me."

"I'd like to see them," he said. As his lips formed the words, he was wondering how she'd feel if she knew the real reason behind his sudden interest, which was to get his hands on a picture of Andrew O'Brien for the FBI. He felt like a scumbag keeping things from her. "Well, I guess I'll let you go. I know you have a lot of things to do. Make sure you call again tomorrow night. I love you."

"I love you," Emilia said and hung up the phone. She walked into the bedroom and found her pictures on the top shelf of the bedroom closet. She felt a growing nostalgia as she sat on the bed and looked through them. There were several pictures of Katherine, Andrew and James with her grandmother Emma. They appeared to be from birth up to about twenty years of age. She smiled. There must have been a camera buff somewhere in the relationship she thought. Emilia put these pictures in her overnight case so she wouldn't forget them.

Emilia awoke the next morning before the alarm went off. Before going to bed, she had cleaned up the apartment a little and taken care of her mail that had accumulated. She planned on packing her suitcase in preparation for the weekend with Brad and Dennis when she got home from work. She yawned as she walked into the bathroom to take a shower and get dressed.

She decided to go to the office early today since she had a meeting to attend in the afternoon. Chuck Collins was a good friend and he needed all the support he could get. She hoped he would be successful in his endeavor to keep those books out of the school library and foil the APLA's attempt to set a precedent here in Plymouth. It didn't take a rocket scientist to figure out their strategy.

She looked out the window and saw that Bill and Howard were both in the car across the street waiting for her. I think I'll take those two to breakfast, she thought as she closed her apartment door.

As Emilia approached the car, Howard got out to open the back door for her.

"Good morning," Emilia said. "How would you two like to join me for breakfast?"

"Sounds good to me," Bill replied. "Where would you like to go?"

"There's a diner right down the street from the office," she said. "It's fast and the food is pretty good. Irene won't be in yet so we'll take some coffee back with us."

They all had the bacon and egg special and were on their way within forty-five minutes. Along with the coffee, they bought doughnuts for later on in the morning.

Emilia noticed that Irene was surprised to find her already there when she came into her office. "Good morning," Irene said. "What happened, did you wet the bed?"

Emilia knew this was the standard office joke for someone who showed up significantly early for work.

Emilia laughed. "No, I didn't. I came in early because of Chuck's meeting this afternoon. I wanted to make sure I got everything cleaned up beforehand in case it turns out to be an all day affair. I'm returning to the Cape first thing tomorrow morning."

Emilia told Irene she would buzz her if she needed anything. She looked through the mail first, and then the phone messages Irene had brought in. She took care of her correspondence and made several phone calls by eleven-thirty.

After lunch, Emilia began getting her things ready for the meeting. She asked Irene to get her a pen and notebook and told her she would be leaving in about fifteen minutes. Emilia made one more phone call then left the office with Bill and Howard.

They got to Plymouth High School at 2:15 and took their seats in the back of the auditorium. A table was set up on the stage for the School Board and their attorney. As it got closer to 2:30, the auditorium began filling up with concerned parents. She noticed one older man coming in who looked vaguely familiar, but she couldn't quite place him. He apparently had the same reaction when their eyes met. Maybe it's déjà vu, she thought. She was surprised to see Chief Archer, who was there with two men she'd never seen before. They were getting quite a crowd, which is what Chuck had hoped for.

The meeting was called to order and Chuck presented a brief opening statement on the American Personal Liberties Association's intention to introduce a series of children's books into their School Library Program. He emphasized that the School Board had already unanimously rejected the books and was now being threatened with a possible lawsuit to bring them into compliance. Since a lawsuit might prove to be costly, they needed a vote of approval before issuing a final rejection with subsequent potential litigation.

Chuck's assistants passed out descriptive literature on the specific contents of the books.

Emilia looked around the room as the people read the literature. The reaction could be seen in their faces. To say it was a look of surprise would be an understatement she thought. She noticed some whose initial blush of embarrassment was slowly turning to a look of anger. The quiet atmosphere, which prevailed while they were reading, was now replaced by exuberant sounds of indignation. Several verbalized their disapproval in no uncertain terms.

It was fortunate for the attorney representing the APLA that security guards were present. Emilia thought he would probably have ended up being tarred and feathered. The crowd would not even afford him the opportunity of speaking. He finally gave up and left the stage.

Chuck Collins then officially took a vote on the issue, which was the appropriate procedure to follow, even though it seemed to be unnecessary. The vote was unanimous.

The next step would be up to the APLA. Emilia was sure they would not back down. She could only hope the court would rule for the Plymouth School District.

As she got her things together and got up to go, she ran into Chief Archer.

Emilia laughed. "This is getting to be a habit. I seem to run into you wherever I go."

"The pleasure is all mine," he said.

She was then introduced to his two companions, Agents Lawson and Bradley, and told they were also in law enforcement. He didn't elaborate on the specific branch. When she started to introduce Bill and Howard, she found they already knew each other.

"Isn't this a small world?" she asked. "There must be a lot of interaction in law enforcement."

"There sure is," Chief Archer said. "What did you think of the meeting?"

"The people reacted the way I thought they would," Emilia said. "What was your impression?"

"I wasn't surprised," he replied. "It's what I expected."

Just then, the older man Emilia had seen earlier stopped directly in front of her. She looked into his eyes and thought she saw a flicker of recognition for just a brief moment. They moved aside so those behind him could get past.

"Have we met before?" she asked. "You look so familiar."

"I feel the same about you," he said. "But I don't believe we have."

"I'm Emilia Wright," she said. "What is your name? Perhaps that will help us remember if we have."

Emilia became aware that Agents Lawson and Bradley seemed unusually interested in this encounter and wondered why.

"My name is Paul Freedman," he said. "Your name is not familiar to me. It's not likely that we've met since I'm not from around these parts. I've always lived in Chicago. I guess you just remind me of someone, maybe from my past."

As she watched him walk away, Emilia realized he resembled someone in the old photographs she looked at last night but she couldn't remember who. She made a mental note to look through them again tonight. She wondered why Chief Archer and his two companions also appeared interested in Paul Freedman. Perhaps the photographs will hold some clue she thought.

Emilia said good-bye to Chief Archer, found Chuck Collins to congratulate him on the outcome of the meeting, then left the auditorium with Bill and Howard. She figured it was too late to bother going back to the office, and there was actually no reason to, so she decided to call it a day. She invited Bill and Howard to have dinner with her at Sam's Seafood on the way home.

It was about eight o'clock and already dark when they pulled up at the apartment complex. When she got out of the car, Emilia told them goodnight and to plan on an early start in the morning.

When she entered her apartment, she noticed the light blinking on the answering machine and assumed it was probably Dennis wondering why she hadn't called yet. When she played it, she could hear the underlying concern in his voice and realized she better call quickly or she'd have him on her doorstep.

When Dennis answered the phone, she said, "Hello, Denny. I'm sorry to be so late."

"That's OK," he said. "I must admit, we were beginning to get a little concerned. You just missed Brad. He went to get a paper. Did you go somewhere after work?"

"I treated Bill and Howard to dinner on the way home. I thought it would save time. I've still got to pack my bag and do a few little things around here. I want to get an early start in the morning. We're sure to hit those weekend pockets of traffic congestion with the official tourist season beginning soon."

"How did the meeting go this afternoon?" Dennis asked.

"It went pretty much as Chuck expected," she said. "I'll fill you in on the details when I see you tomorrow. The next move will be up to the APLA."

"I suppose it was over rather quickly."

"It sure was. Speaking of the meeting, you just reminded me of a gentleman I met there who looked like someone in those old photographs I was looking through last night. If I have time, I'm going to look at them again."

"Well, I won't hold you up," he said. "I'll see you in the morning. I'm so anxious to see you, I won't be able to sleep. Love you."

"And I love you," she said and hung up.

Emilia went into the kitchen to make a cup of tea before getting started. Most of the photographs were still on the table and she hoped to scan through them before putting them away.

It didn't take her long to pack, water the plants and clean up the apartment. She then began her search through the old photographs for the picture of the man who resembled Paul Freedman.

She found it was the one of her grandmother Emma with Katherine, James and Andrew. He clearly resembled one of the boys, even though he was much older now, but she still wasn't sure which was James and which was Andrew. It was a duplicate of one of the pictures she already had in her case to show Dennis and she was sure Brad would be able to tell them apart.

~ FIFTEEN ~

Jeff heard the phone ringing, but his head was throbbing and he couldn't get up to answer. When he'd called the doctor's office this morning for an appointment, he was told the earliest they could squeeze him in would be tomorrow morning at nine o'clock. He was told if the pain became too severe, he should go to the emergency room for treatment.

He realized the time lapses he couldn't account for when he suddenly lost touch with reality were becoming more frequent. Fortunately, he was always alone when they occurred. The thought of losing control was frightening to him, especially since he worked so hard to reach his current position.

He was aghast at the possibility that he wouldn't live long enough to witness his lifelong ambition of destroying Brad and his family. It was too bad Katherine wasn't around to know. It wasn't fair of her to go before he'd completed the job.

He wouldn't allow this sickness to stop him. He had planned his revenge against Brad for years. He refused to be deprived of the anticipated gratification. The abduction of Emilia Wright would be the final and worst impact on Brad, much more than losing money or suffering a maligned reputation.

His head was pounding as he finally passed out.

When he awoke again, he looked at the clock and saw that it was nine o'clock. His headache had subsided and he was able to think again. In spite of the pain, he was pretty sure he'd heard Paul on the answering machine. He groped his way into the kitchen to put on some coffee. When he turned on the light, the brightness made him wince with pain as he felt a knife-like sensation hit his eyes. He knew he would need some aspirin and a cup of coffee before he could return Paul's call for a report on the school board meeting.

After he turned on the coffeepot, he went into the bathroom and splashed some water on his face and dried it very carefully with a soft towel. He looked at his reflection in the mirror above the sink. He was startled at how drawn his face looked.

He went back to the kitchen and got a cup of coffee. As he sipped the coffee, Jeff realized he would soon have to make a decision about Paul. In the interim, he decided to deal directly with the two men Paul hired to kidnap Emilia. Jeff realized he would have to get their names again when he called Paul.

In a way, Jeff was sure he would miss Paul; as much as he was capable of missing anyone. Sometimes he felt such a profound sadness at his lack of any sincere relationship with anyone, including his own daughter and grandchildren. Living a double life, as he did, precluded any such relationship he told himself. But growing older began to soften his resolve and he often wished there were more in his life.

He gently massaged his head and tried to remember when his hatred of Brad first began. It must have been more than sibling rivalry but he couldn't remember any specific circumstance that he could put his finger on. He only knew it was all consuming and constant. In a way, he looked forward to the day when Brad was aware of it and he would no longer have to feign brotherly love, although of late he did little to conceal his feelings.

Even the realization that he would be required to make recompense someday for the things he did, either in this world or the next, did not invoke any sense of penance. He felt no remorse or any pangs of conscience. He understood that most people would consider him hopeless.

These bouts of self analysis usually left him feeling depressed. He shrugged the feeling off and dialed Paul's number.

Jeff detected annoyance in Paul's voice when he answered but he could care less.

"How did the meeting go?" Jeff asked. "Did you take notes and make a report?"

"I took notes at the meeting," Paul replied. "I started writing the report after dinner tonight but I haven't quite finished it yet. I'll have it for you tomorrow."

"That's good enough," Jeff said. "I'm sure we'll end up in court again."

"I think so," Paul said. "Do you want me to bring it over in the morning?"

"No, I have an appointment in the morning," Jeff replied. "I'll give you a call when I get home. By the way, what are the names of the two men you sent back to the Cape for me?"

"Jake Powell and Carl Matthews," Paul replied. "Is there something wrong?"

"No," Jeff replied. "I just wondered. I'll see you tomorrow."

"All right," Paul said. "Good night."

Jeff knew his headache was beginning again by the pain in his temples. Soon it would spread to encompass his whole head, which would then pound and throb like an abscessed tooth. As he headed for the bed, he was so glad he made an appointment to see the doctor in the morning. He was optimistic the doctor would be able to make an educated diagnosis without first exposing him to a battery of tests. But that would indeed be a rarity in this day and age when doctors paid huge insurance premiums to cover lawsuits they incurred for being wrong he thought. He hoped the extra aspirin he took before he called Paul would give him some relief so he could get some sleep.

Jeff awoke again at two o'clock. He decided to place the call to Jake Powell regardless of the time. The phone rang about ten times before Jake answered.

"Hello," he mumbled not quite awake.

"Jake, this is Jeff Owensford. Do you recognize the name?"

"Yes, sir," Jake was suddenly wide-awake. "Paul works for you."

"That's right," Jeff said. "I'm calling you personally because Paul is tied up on a special assignment; therefore, you will be dealing directly with me until further notice. Any questions?"

"No, sir," Jake replied. "I'm at your disposal."

"Good," Jeff said. "The reason you were sent back to Plymouth is because there's something I want done tomorrow morning. And this time, I don't want any mistakes. Emilia Wright will be heading to the Cape early in the morning and I'm giving you another chance to abduct her and keep her out of commission until I give you further instructions. If you fail this time, your services will no longer be required. Is that understood?"

"Yes, sir, that's quite clear," Jake said. "Don't worry, we won't fail this time. Will she be alone?"

Jeff laughed. He lit a cigarette before he answered. "That's up to you. She has two bodyguards who have been accompanying her everywhere. If you're able to put them out of commission before she leaves in the morning, then she'll be alone. If not, they will be with her. I really don't care how you arrange it as long as it gets done." Jeff took a deep drag on his cigarette.

"We'll handle it," Jake said. "Do you still want her taken to the boat on the canal?"

"Yes," Jeff replied. "Come to think of it, I don't think anyone knows I have a boat there. It's been years since I've used it, although I make sure it's kept in good running order in case I ever decide to sell it. Just give me a call and let me know when the job's done. I have an appointment early in the morning, but I hope to be home by noon."

Jeff took one more long drag on his cigarette, then ground it out in the ashtray on his nightstand and turned over to try to go back to sleep.

As he tossed and turned, he thought back on his life and wondered what it would be like to be given a second chance. He wondered what he would do differently. Perhaps he wouldn't introduce Brad to Katherine.

Come to think of it, Brad is really to blame for everything that happened to me since he thought. But soon the tables will turn. I will have Brad on his knees before I am through with him. Ah, revenge will be so sweet he thought as he drifted into a fitful sleep.

Jeff Owensford's appointment was for nine o'clock and he arrived at the doctor's office about ten minutes early. He hadn't had a physical examination for about three years and was expecting a lecture on the merits of preventive medicine because of his procrastination. He hoped the extreme pain he suffered might inhibit the anticipated discourse.

They called him promptly and, following the routine weight and blood pressure screening, he was shown into a small examination room. Jeff stepped up and sat down on the end of the examination table minutes before Dr. Scott entered the room.

Dr. Scott shook Jeff's hand. "How are you this morning?" he asked. "Your chart indicates you're here because of a problem with recurring headaches."

"That's right," Jeff said. "When they first began, they weren't as bad nor as frequent as they are now. A few times, I experienced a time lapse where I couldn't remember anything."

"How long did these periods last?" Dr. Scott asked.

"Maybe an hour or so," Jeff replied. "I'm not really sure."

"Were you always alone when these attacks occurred and do you have any idea what precipitated them?"

"Fortunately I was always alone, and I don't have any idea why they happened," Jeff said. "I am quite concerned and lately the pain has become unbearable."

Dr. Scott checked Jeff's ears to rule out any infection there, and then examined his eyes with a light. He said everything appeared to be normal. Then Dr. Scott told Jeff to stand up facing him and follow his instructions. First he had him put his arms out to the side, then first with his right hand, and then with his left, he told him to touch the tip of his nose. Then, as the doctor moved his finger left to right, then up and down, Jeff was told to follow these movements with his eyes. Jeff had no problem following and completing any of the instructions. Then Dr. Scott asked Jeff to show him exactly where the pain was located.

"Tell me, do you have any nausea with these episodes?" Dr. Scott asked.

"Sometimes I do, but not always," Jeff replied. "What do you think it is?"

"I'm not able to make any determination from this preliminary examination," Dr. Scott replied. "You're not exhibiting any of the classic symptoms normally associated with brain tumor or concussion. It could be the onset of migraine headaches. Believe me, they can be very severe in some instances. Another possibility might be emotional stress. The time lapses are what I'm particularly concerned about. I think it would be appropriate to order an MRI test before proceeding any further. It's the only way to rule out any serious disorder."

"If I have to get one, could it be done as soon as possible?" Jeff asked. "I have some very urgent business coming up."

"We can arrange for you to get it later this morning," Dr. Scott said.

"How long does it take to get the results?" Jeff asked.

"I'll try to have them for you tomorrow," he replied. "In the meantime, I'll write a prescription for the pain. To be most effective, this medication should be taken at the first sign of an impending headache, rather than after it builds to a crescendo. You can go out in the waiting room now and I'll have the nurse make arrangements for your test. She'll let you know where and what time. Take care and give us a call tomorrow afternoon."

"Thank you," Jeff said. "I'll talk to you tomorrow."

The nurse made an appointment for Jeff at General Hospital for 10:45. He decided to get his prescription filled and go right over. Perhaps if he got there early, they would take him sooner, he thought.

- SIXTEEN -

Emilia left her apartment at six o'clock and crossed the street to where Howard and Bill were waiting for her in the car. Howard got out of the passenger side of the front seat to open the back door for her and they immediately pulled away.

"Good morning," Emilia said. "How are you this morning?"

"Just fine," Howard said. "Looks like it's going to be a nice day. Are we going straight through?"

"No, I think we'll stop for breakfast," she replied. "I don't want to get there before they're up."

"Any place in particular?" Bill asked.

"We'll stop at the Thomasville Inn," she replied. "It's right before the bridge that crosses over to the Cape. We'll probably be there in about fifteen minutes."

The Thomasville Inn opened at 6:00 a.m. It was apparent that the customers, only a handful, were professional people, probably stopping for breakfast on their way to work. The service was good and they were on their way in less than an hour.

The traffic was light as they crossed the bridge to the Cape and they proceeded along Route 6A until they came to the turn off, a private road, which she remembered Dennis said was approximately two or three miles from Brad's house.

As they drove along the private road, Emilia noticed Bill and Howard stopped talking and seemed to be especially observant. She sensed that they were apprehensive and she understood why. The road to Brad's house was not well traveled, very winding and quite isolated, with only woods lining the road on both sides.

Then, just up ahead, Emilia saw a tree down, blocking the road, and was immediately filled with dread. She heard Bill yell, "Brace yourself." He slammed on the brakes and then tried to maneuver the car around. Emilia heard a shot ring out. Bill slumped over the wheel and she saw blood gush from a deep gaping wound on the side of his head.

Emilia screamed as Howard drew his gun. He reached back and pushed her to the floor of the car. "Stay down," he yelled. She watched through the opening between the front seats and saw him try to move Bill over so he could get behind the wheel. As Howard struggled to move Bill, she heard another shot and Howard fell back against the door. Emilia screamed in horror when she realized both Howard and Bill had been shot.

She didn't know what to do. Her only thought was to get help. She stretched forward and over Bill in the front seat and leaned on the horn. Then she saw the two men come out from behind the trees and look up and down the road.

She opened the car door, jumped out and ran down the road. She could hear them running behind her and she knew they were gaining. Her legs were numb as though they were wooden and belonged to someone else. She was gasping for air and felt as though her heart would burst if she didn't stop. She stumbled and turned her ankle. When she tried to run again, she felt a hand grab her arm. She tried to pull away and couldn't. Her arm felt like it was in a vise. Then the other man caught up and she screamed hysterically as the two of them tried to hold her and keep her from running.

Then Emilia felt something over her nose and mouth. She could taste and smell something sweet and pungent. Her limbs became heavy and she had a sensation of falling. Then there was nothing but darkness.

Much later, as Emilia struggled to regain consciousness, she had no immediate recollection of what happened. All her effort was concentrated on trying to focus and wake up. Why am I having such a hard time waking up, she thought? Her memory flashed back to a time when she was in the hospital and how hard she struggled to come out of an anesthetic.

She groaned. Her nose and throat felt raw and her head throbbed. When she tried to move her head, a wave of dizziness swept over her and left her nauseous. Then she tried to move and felt something holding her down, and the panic rose up in her throat. The only reality that existed was the panic and the silent screams. Something was holding her and she couldn't move. There was no other thought. She was hysterical, and all she could hear was the thunderous beat of her heart, and she knew she was going to die. As the fight-or-flight mechanism went into high gear, Emilia was at the height of perception and wide-awake.

Knowing it was the panic associated with agoraphobia had little impact. It was a long time since she'd gone to therapy and learned the relaxation rituals and breathing exercises, which had all but eliminated the symptoms. In therapy she learned that being able to function well in the world was the ultimate goal of an agoraphobic, and she had become quite successful in this regard. But she had never been put to such a violent test.

Oh, God, please help me, she thought. Please give me the strength that passeth all human understanding. It was a verse she used numerous times during her therapy. She knew she must try to remain calm. She took a deep breath, held it, and slowly let it out.

As she concentrated on her breathing, something touched her shoulder. She opened her eyes and all the horror came back. Looking down at her was one of the men who had shot Bill and Howard. It was he and another man who had chased and caught her. She realized that it must have been chloroform that was held over her face. That's why she couldn't wake up. She flinched at his touch and could feel the panic about to well up again inside her. All her senses told her she must try to fight it and remain calm, but she didn't know if she could.

Emilia knew he saw the sheer terror in her eyes when he looked at her like she was some wild animal who was trapped and cornered. She thought he actually looked worried at the possibility that she might literally be scared to death.

"If you promise not to scream, I'll take the gag out of your mouth," he said. "You don't have to be afraid. I'm not going to hurt you."

Emilia nodded her head and he removed the gag.

"Please untie me," Emilia cried. "I'll do whatever you say. Only please untie me. You don't understand. I have this phobia and I can't stand to be held down. Oh, please, untie me."

She knew he was thinking it over. Emilia didn't know if he was aware of such phobias, but she sensed he realized that the terror he saw in her eyes stemmed from much more than being afraid of him. She hoped he would also understand that he could untie her and she wouldn't try to run for fear of being tied up again.

"All right," he said. "I'll untie you. But if you try to escape, I'll have to tie you up again, and keep you tied up until this is over."

After he untied her, Emilia went limp with relief. She thought of nothing but the relief until she suddenly remembered the danger, which still confronted her. She was afraid to speak; she might say something that would antagonize him.

He helped her sit up. "Is that better?" he asked.

"Yes, thank you," she replied. Her throat was so raw it hurt to swallow. And she was still very lightheaded. She was on some sort of cot against the wall.

"Would you like some coffee and something to eat?" he asked. "It will make you feel better."

"Yes, I'd like some coffee," Emilia said. "I'm not hungry. In fact, I feel a little nauseous."

"That's from the chloroform," he said. "It might effect you for three or four days. If you try a little toast, it might help."

"All right," she said. "I'll try." So it was chloroform she thought, and wondered where they got it. She looked around as he made her toast. It looked and felt like she was on some sort of boat, probably a large one judging from the size of the cabin. He put her toast and coffee on a small table, which was in front of the cot.

He had been right. She did feel better after she ate the toast. As she sipped her coffee, the other man came down into the cabin. It was evident from their conversation that the one who untied her was the one in charge. She didn't like the looks of either one.

Emilia wondered about Bill and Howard, and whether they were dead or alive. She prayed they were found in time. She felt the hot tears run down her cheeks and quickly wiped them away before the kidnappers noticed.

"Look, you just relax down here," he said. "We're going up on deck for a while."

Emilia wondered how annoyed he would be if she asked a question. So far, he had acted in a civilized manner toward her and she figured he would keep the other one in line. She didn't believe they were going to harm her, at least not for now.

"What do you plan to do with me?" she asked.

"I already told you we're not going to hurt you," he said. "Keeping you out of circulation is what we were hired to do. There's nothing personal."

"But how long are you going to keep me here?" she asked.

He laughed. "I don't even know the answer to that one," he replied. "Now that's enough questions."

Emilia knew better than to persist. All she could do was hope and pray that Dennis would find her. She knew that by now he must be frantic and already searching for her.

~ SEVENTEEN ~

As Emilia had anticipated, a massive search was already under way. When she failed to arrive at Brad's house by nine o'clock and they couldn't get her on the phone, Dennis immediately notified Chief Archer.

He then checked with security at her apartment complex and verified that she left the building at six o'clock. Once he confirmed this, he placed a call to Agent Lawson. He was not in and Dennis left a message before leaving Brad's house to conduct the investigation first-hand. He asked Brad to remain at the house in case Emilia showed up. Dennis realized he must try to put his personal feelings aside, hard as it might be, so he wouldn't hinder the investigation.

As he drove along the road toward Route 6A, he came to the spot where the tree lay across the road. He recognized the car on the other side of the tree as the one Emilia's bodyguards were using. It was turned sideways as though they had been trying to turn around. There was no sign of anyone. Just as he was getting out of the car to investigate, he noticed Agents Lawson and Bradley pull up. He watched as they drew their guns and approached the car. Then he saw them holster their guns as they looked into the front seat.

Dennis ran over to the car, his heart in his throat, to see what they found. He looked into the front seat with mixed feelings. It was apparent that Bill and Howard had both been shot. Howard was slouched up against the door on the passenger side of the seat and groaned as Steve touched him. There was blood on the side of his head but the wound did not appear to be deep, rather as though he'd been grazed. Agent Lawson helped him to sit up.

Then Dennis looked at Bill who was slumped over toward the opposite door. He lay motionless as Agent Lawson felt for a pulse. "He's still breathing," he shouted to Agent Bradley. "Get on the radio and get an ambulance out here quick."

As Agent Lawson worked on Bill, Dennis ran over to Howard. "Who did it?" he asked.

"I don't know," Howard replied. "We never saw them."

"Do you know what happened to Emilia?" Dennis asked. "We don't see her anywhere around. Only her purse is in the back seat." Dennis could see Howard was still dazed.

"Whoever shot us must have taken her," Howard said. "What about Bill? Is he all right?"

"I don't know," Dennis replied. "He's got a pretty bad wound on the side of his head. An ambulance is on the way." Dennis heard Agent Lawson say that they would probably fly Bill into the trauma center in Boston. Dennis asked Howard exactly what happened.

"When we realized it was a trap, Bill slammed on the brakes and tried to turn the car around to get away," Howard said. "That's when he was shot. After I pushed Miss Wright down on the floor in the back, I tried to move Bill out of the driver's seat. That's the last thing I remember. The shots must have come from the woods on the side of the road where they knew we would have to stop."

Just then, Agent Bradley joined them. "Did you find anything?" Dennis asked.

"It looks like Miss Wright jumped out of the car and ran," Agent Bradley said. "There's a spot, several yards from the car, where it looks like a scuffle took place when they caught up with her. I also found a square of material with the distinct scent of chloroform."

Dennis felt as though he'd been hit in the stomach with a fist. "I think we better call and let Chief Archer know that we found the car and Emilia is missing," he said. "The fact that they used chloroform to subdue her might be a good sign that they don't intend to harm her."

"I hope so," Agent Bradley said. "I'd hate to see anything happen to her. She seems to be a very nice person."

"Yes, she is," Dennis said. "I know she's smart enough to play along and do as they say. She'll know that everyone will be out looking for her. It will just be a matter of time before we find her, even if we have to turn the whole town upside down to do it."

Just then Dennis saw the ambulance arrive. He watched as the paramedics quickly put Bill into the ambulance and headed down the road. Then Agent Lawson came over and joined them. "Could this have anything to do with Paul Freedman being at the school board meeting?" Dennis asked. "He must be the guy who looked so familiar to Emilia."

"You said she told you the man appeared to recognize her for a moment?" Agent Lawson asked. "It could mean that with the proper stimulus he might regain his memory."

"Wouldn't that be dangerous for him?" Dennis asked. "You implied Jeff was keeping him around to insure that he didn't remember."

"That's right," Agent Lawson said. "He would be signing his own death warrant. Jeff would have no other choice than to get rid of him as he once tried to years ago. If there's no doubt that it's Andrew O'Brien, we may decide to reveal to Brad Owensford what we know about his brother. You've known him for years. How do you think he'll react?"

"He already knows Jeff barely tolerates him," Dennis said. "I think he'll find it hard to believe. He will undoubtedly think of various reasons why your information must be incorrect. If that fails, he will begin creating excuses for Jeff's behavior. Brad is a very unique person and family means a great deal to him."

Dennis realized what they didn't want was Paul's restored memory to serve as a warning to Jeff of possible apprehension by the FBI. Jeff is no dummy he thought. He would know exactly how much harm Paul could accomplish by what he knew. Dennis listened as Agent Lawson explained the FBI's projection in the case.

"Our first and foremost objective is the complete elimination of the APLA, whose primary financial backing is the direct result of Jeff Owensford's blackmail of his brother, Brad Owensford," Agent Lawson said. "What we need is conclusive evidence, which would substantiate several theories about Jeff Owensford's criminal involvement in attempted murder. Then we could confidently file charges that would lead to a conviction. Without the surety of conviction, we might be giving him an opportunity to destroy any documentation which we could use to prove his participation in the organization."

Dennis understood now why they felt they might have to tell Brad about Jeff. He wondered what Brad's reaction would be if they did..

Dennis got back to Brad's house about 10:30 and found him pacing the floor, filled with anxiety and understandable disbelief that anything could have happened to Emilia. He found Brad inconsolable in his own sense of guilt at not preventing this occurrence. Dennis knew it would only get worse when he heard the latest. He noticed Brad's demeanor change when he turned and saw him. Dennis sensed he was prepared to receive good news and steeled against bad.

"I think Emilia has been kidnapped," Dennis said. He saw the color drain from Brad's face as he dropped into the nearest chair.

"How could this happen?" Brad asked. "Where were her bodyguards?"

"They've both been shot," Dennis said. "Howard's wound looked superficial but Bill appeared to be critical."

"Where did it happen?" Brad asked.

"It happened on your private road to the house, about one and one-half miles from Route 6A. There was a tree down across the road and when Bill, who was driving and realized it was a trap, tried to turn the car around he was shot. Howard was shot as he tried to move Bill out of the driver's seat."

Brad interrupted. "Then why are you so sure Emilia was kidnapped?" Brad asked. "She might have run into the woods and gotten away." Dennis could see that Brad was hoping that by some miracle Emilia had gotten away.

"There were indications of a scuffle several yards from the car, which leads me to believe that Emilia was seized while attempting to run away. There was also a cloth at the scene that smelled of chloroform, which I think was used to render her unconscious." Dennis was aware by the look of resignation on Brad's face that he now accepted the fact that Emilia had been abducted.

"How will we find her?" Brad asked. "What's being done?"

"A massive search is already underway," Dennis said. "We'll find her."

"But what if we don't find her in time?" Brad asked with anguish in his voice.

"We will find her," Dennis said. "If I personally have to turn this town upside down, I promise you I will find her." Dennis suddenly felt anger surge through him like a hot fire as the initial shock began to fade. "Just remember one thing," he said. "They have no intention of hurting her. That would jeopardize the leverage they now enjoy."

"We've got to find out who's behind all this," Brad said.

Dennis knew that Agents Lawson and Bradley would soon be here with precisely the information Brad wanted, but it was not going to be what he wanted to hear.

"I'm sure we will," Dennis said. "Keep in mind, knowing who's behind it will not give you any advantage right now. They will still hold the upper hand, and they will until we can find out where they've taken her." Dennis sat down in the chair next to Brad. He leaned his head back and closed his eyes. All he could think of was Emilia. He wondered if she had been hurt. He was unaccustomed to the savage rage he felt, which was directed toward whomever was responsible. He opened his eyes as Brad handed him a glass of iced tea.

"Perhaps we could deal with them," Brad suggested. "I'll give whatever they want to get her back."

"I'm sure they're counting on that," Dennis said.

"There must be something we can do," Brad said. "I just can't sit here doing nothing. I'll go crazy." Dennis drank his tea while Brad commenced to pace back and forth across the room.

"Let's wait and see what Agent Lawson has to say," Dennis said. "I thought he and Agent Bradley would be here by now. I think I'll go back down the road and see what's holding them up."

"I'll go with you," Brad said.

"You better stay here by the phone," Dennis said as he walked toward the door. "I'll come right back and let you know what's going on."

Dennis got in his car and started down the road. As he neared the spot where it happened, he saw that Agents Lawson and Bradley were still there. They waited at the scene while the forensic team retrieved fingerprints, blood samples and any other pertinent evidence available. Agent Lawson told Dennis they examined the contents of Emilia's handbag and found a photograph they wanted to show Brad

Owensford. Dennis wondered if the photograph would turn out to be another piece of the puzzle.

Dennis heard that Howard's wound was superficial as they thought, but Bill was listed in critical condition. "I sure hope Bill makes it," he said.

"The two guys who shot him better hope he does, too," Agent Lawson said. "We are going to get them. I don't care how long it takes."

"I feel the same," Agent Bradley said.

"It worries me sick that the likes of them have Emilia," Dennis said. "When we find them, we'll have to use caution so she doesn't get hurt."

"That goes without saying," Agent Lawson said. "They would feel no compulsion against killing her if it afforded them an opportunity to get away."

The forensic team finished up a few minutes later and Brad's car, which the bodyguards had been using, was towed away. Dennis got in his car, put the window down, and asked Agents Lawson and Bradley if they planned on coming back to the house now. They nodded yes and got in their car to follow him. When they arrived, they found Brad out on the back deck randomly turning the pages of the morning paper. Dennis saw Brad look up expectantly as they came out onto the deck.

"I'm sorry, there's nothing yet." Dennis said. He noticed the look of expectation change to one of disappointment.

"I assure you we'll have people working round the clock on it," Agent Lawson said.

"Then you think it's going to take some time?" Brad asked.

"They have quite a bit of area to cover," Dennis said. "She could be anywhere on the Cape."

"There's coffee on the table if you'd like some," Brad said. "Please sit down and help yourself."

"Sounds good," Agent Bradley said as the three sat down with Brad at the table. As they got their coffee, Agent Bradley continued. "We're going to have your telephone tapped after lunch. Just a precaution in the event they call you with specific demands." Dennis had expected them to tap Brad's phone. He watched as Agent Lawson took the photograph out of his pocket and handed it to Brad.

"We found this in Emilia's handbag," he said. "Thought it might mean something to you." Dennis sipped his coffee as Brad studied the picture.

"It's a picture of Emilia's grandmother with her three children, Katherine, James and Andrew," Brad said. "I wonder why she had that with her?"

"I think I know," Dennis said. "Emilia told me there was a man at the meeting she attended yesterday afternoon who resembled someone in the old family photographs she looked through the night before. She planned on going through them again last night to see if she could find the picture. I think this is probably the one she was looking for."

"Well, I think we have the answer to one piece of the puzzle," Agent Lawson said.

"Then your suspicion that Paul Freedman is really Andrew O'Brien must be true," Dennis said. "But he'll be of little help unless he happens to regain his memory."

"I don't understand," Brad interrupted. "I thought Andrew O'Brien disappeared many years ago. I heard about it when I returned from Europe."

"He's had amnesia all these years," Dennis said. "When he and Emilia saw each other at the meeting, they both felt a sense of recognition. Nothing registered for either one at hearing the other's name because Andrew has a fictitious name and Emilia's name was not a familiar one from his past."

"That is so unbelievable," Brad said. "After all these years."

"Yes, it certainly is," Dennis agreed. "It might prove to be dangerous for Andrew." He then asked Agent Lawson to tell Brad what the FBI's investigation had revealed about Paul Freedman.

"His amnesia is the result of a severe beating he received when he first arrived in Chicago," Agent Lawson said. "His amnesia is, without a doubt, the only plausible explanation for why they didn't finish the job. He was no threat as long as he couldn't remember what happened."

"A threat to whom?" Brad asked. "I don't understand what Katherine's brother, Andrew O'Brien, could possibly have to do with all this." Dennis noticed that Brad looked anxious and absolutely bewildered. He looked over at Agent Lawson and wondered if he also saw the effect that all this was having on Brad. He didn't wait long to find out.

"I don't want to go into the whole thing just yet," Agent Lawson said. "Let's wait until we have Miss Wright safely back. The rest of it can wait until then."

Dennis realized Agent Lawson was not going to inform Brad about Jeff at this particular time. He sensed that Agent Lawson could also see, after careful observation, it was dubious whether Brad could sustain another emotional shock without suffering any physical consequences. He told Brad he'd be back to see him later.

Dennis could see that Brad was distraught as they watched the noon news. He was filled with compassion for him because he too experienced the mixed feeling of helplessness and guilt that he saw tearing Brad apart.

Then there was the big word IF to deal with. IF we hadn't let her go back to Plymouth, IF we had gone with her, IF we had provided more protection, and on, and on.

Oh, Emilia, Dennis thought. Please be all right. Oh, God please let her be all right.

Later in the afternoon as Dennis sat down to watch the news, the phone rang and he immediately recognized Chief Archer's voice.

"Yes," Dennis said. "Is there some news of Emilia?"

"No, nothing yet," Chief Archer said. "Has there been any demand made yet? We've got the phone tapped so we know there was nothing there."

"No, we haven't heard a thing," Dennis said. "You'd think they would have contacted Brad by now. I wonder what they're waiting for? I can't remember when I've put in such a long day. You feel so helpless when there's nothing you can do."

"I understand," Chief Archer said. "We all feel the same way. All we can do is wait until they make the next move. How is Mr. Owensford holding up?"

"He's doing pretty good," Dennis said. "At first, I thought he might become a basket case. He's taking a walk on the beach right now. I think he wanted to be alone for a while."

"Well, I'll let you go," Chief Archer said. "Perhaps tomorrow will bring good news."

"I hope so," Dennis said.

After Dennis hung up, he walked out to the deck and sat down to wait for Brad to return. He didn't wait long before he heard Brad coming up the steps. "How was the walk?" Dennis asked. "Did it help?"

"It calmed me down a little," Brad said. "I thought it might help me to sleep tonight."

"You better get some sleep," Dennis said. "They might need you and if you're suffering from sleep depravation, you won't be worth too much."

"You're right," Brad said. "I think I'll go upstairs right after dinner."

"I think I'll turn in early too," Dennis said. "There are a few things I want to check out tomorrow morning. I'm sure Chief Archer will call if he hears anything."

- *EIGHTEEN* -

Jeff felt a little shaky as his head was put into the cylinder for his MRI test. He received instructions beforehand to make him aware that the banging noise he heard was standard. As the test progressed, he thought if he didn't have a headache before it began, he was sure to have one by the time it was over. Jeff had a particular problem with laying still and not moving. Finally it ended and he was told his doctor would call him with the results.

Jeff left the hospital and went right home. He entered his apartment, closed the door and walked directly to the answering machine to see if Jake Powell called. As he played back the first message, he heard Jake say that they achieved success in their second attempt and he would call again early this evening. Jeff smiled with delight at the news. He lit a cigarette and went into the kitchen to put the coffee on. While he sat at the kitchen table to wait for the coffee, he thought about the next move in his kidnapping scheme. He wanted to decide before Jake called back for further instructions. He took several deep drags on his cigarette and blew smoke rings while he thought about it.

When the coffee was done, Jeff poured himself a cup and walked back into the living room. He sat down on the recliner and put his coffee on the table beside him. He picked up the remote control and turned on the TV for the noon news. He was just in time to hear the breaking story about the abduction of Emilia Wright, including a visual of an up-to-date photograph. He noticed that Emilia was quite attractive as he listened to the reporter say that the FBI and local authorities asked for the public's assistance in their search for her. He laughed when he heard that the FBI had no leads at the present time but were confident of apprehending the assailants. Jeff sipped his coffee while he listened. During the course of the abduction, the reporter indicated that Emilia's two bodyguards were shot. One was already treated and released from the hospital while the other remained in critical condition. Then as usual, Jeff heard that an update was anticipated for the evening news.

Jeff was pleased to hear about Emilia, but annoyed about the shootings. He didn't care about the victims, but the FBI's efforts to find the assailants would be intensified because of it.

He realized he needed someone with more intelligence than Jake Powell possessed to oversee the operation. Jeff wanted someone whose incentive was not purely mercenary. He needed someone who felt obligated to him and Paul Freedman fit the bill perfectly. Jeff knew the obligation Paul felt toward him for saving his life was the governing factor in Paul's life. Jeff decided to promise retirement, which he knew Paul was after anyway, as an additional inducement for compliance with his request for help.

Jeff decided to think about it later. He was too tired now. He went into the kitchen and made a cup of soup so he wouldn't be taking his capsules for pain on an empty stomach. After he ate, he took his pills, smoked another cigarette, went into the bedroom to lay across the bed and promptly fell asleep.

Jeff opened his eyes and rolled over to see the time and get a cigarette off the nightstand. He noticed it was two o'clock as he stretched and then sat on the side of the bed while he lit his cigarette. The prescription the doctor gave him worked very well to eliminate the pain associated with his headache. He woke up with a clear head and felt stronger and more refreshed than he had in days.

His first thought was to call Paul to make sure he was available in case he decided to send him to the Cape. As he dialed the phone, he wondered if Paul watched the noon news and knew about Emilia. He had better be prepared for the inevitable question of why Jeff called Jake himself.

When Paul answered the phone, Jeff breathed a sigh of relief. Jeff sensed Paul was expecting his call since he didn't sound surprised at hearing his voice. Then he remembered Paul was waiting for a call to deliver the report on the Plymouth School Board Meeting, which Jeff completely forgot about. That will be my excuse to get him over here he thought.

"Yes," Paul said. "Do you want me to bring the report over now?"

"Yes, I'm ready for it," Jeff replied. "How soon can you get here?"

"In about fifteen minutes," Paul said. "Remember, I also asked you yesterday if we could discuss my retirement when I come over."

"Of course, I remember," Jeff said. "We'll talk about that, too. See you in about fifteen minutes."

Jeff knew that Paul wanted to discuss his retirement, which might prove to be the incentive to obtain his cooperation in dealing with Emilia. Then Jeff thought of another motive that might prove to be even stronger. He could say he was sending Paul to make certain Emilia would not be hurt. Jeff knew Paul would accept that reasoning since he knew Jake and Carl personally and understood the lengths to which they would stoop to accomplish their assigned mission.

As Jeff formulated responses to the various arguments he expected to hear from Paul, the telephone rang. Jeff frowned with annoyance when he heard Joyce on the other end. She said she was calling to see if he was all right and to invite him for the weekend. He refused and informed her she would have to excuse him; he had to get some papers ready for someone he was expecting any minute. He promised to call her later.

Jeff no sooner hung up than the doorbell rang. He went over, opened the door for Paul, and invited him to come in and sit down. Jeff took the report Paul handed him as Paul sat down in a chair nearest the door. Jeff made himself a drink and offered one to Paul who refused. Jeff then sat down on the sofa with his drink in one hand and a cigarette in the other. He noticed Paul looked a little nervous.

"How are you, Paul?" Jeff asked. "I haven't actually seen you for a while. You're looking well."

"I'm fine," Paul replied. "How are you?" Jeff didn't miss the surprised look on Paul's face when he first came in. He knew Paul noticed how drawn he looked.

"I'm feeling better," Jeff said. "I was having trouble with headaches. In fact, I saw the doctor only this morning and had an MRI test. From his preliminary examination, he doesn't believe it's anything serious. He thinks it might be the beginning of migraine headaches. He didn't seem particularly concerned."

"That's good news," Paul said. "I guess Joyce is worried about you?"

"I guess she is," Jeff conceded. "I just talked to her on the phone before you arrived." Jeff quickly changed the subject.

"How is Janet?" he asked. "And the children?"

"They're all fine," Paul replied. "Jeff, I don't mean to cut you short, but I would like to talk about my retirement." For the first time, Jeff realized that Paul somehow had summoned the courage to speak up for himself, even though Jeff could see it was with great effort. Will surprises never cease he thought?

"All right," Jeff said. "I have only one favor to ask you before you retire. It's something that I just can't entrust to anyone else. If you handle this for me, you can write off any obligation you've ever felt toward me. That's how important this is."

"What is it you want me to do?" Paul asked. Jeff heard the reluctance in his voice and sensed by the look on his face that Paul had a premonition that it was something to do with Emilia. Jeff knew he would have to be very persuasive as he tried to talk Paul into going to the Cape.

"I may want you to oversee Emilia and make sure she doesn't come to any harm," Jeff replied. "I'm sure you've heard about her abduction on the news. There's a massive search underway at this very moment." Jeff saw the beads of sweat appear on Paul's forehead as he struggled to find his voice.

"Yes, I have heard," Paul said. "I really don't want to get involved in it. I'd already made up my mind that this prior assignment was to be the last. Janet and I have agreed on this." Paul got up and walked over to the window and kept his back to Jeff.

Jeff could see that Paul was becoming more uncomfortable by the minute and figured he better back off a bit. He lit another cigarette and didn't say anything for a few minutes to allow Paul time to calm down. He had the feeling Paul was as close as he'd ever been to refusing to do what Jeff ordered.

"I thought as much," Jeff said. "I promise I won't call on you unless I feel it's absolutely necessary. You don't want to be responsible for her being hurt by Jake and Carl, do you? You're the only one I can trust to assist me by making sure that doesn't happen." Jeff knew his strategy wasn't working when he didn't get any response from Paul. I've got to make him some offer he can't refuse he thought. Then Jeff hit on exactly what it would be.

"Paul, it'll mean an additional $50,000 in your account as a retirement bonus." Jeff said. The sum offered was what Jeff quickly calculated Paul might need for his retirement home. He sensed that Paul was weighing the pros and cons of his proposal. As he pretended to read the report Paul brought, Jeff was aware of the struggle some men face with their own conscience. He was glad he wasn't burdened with such nonsense.

"You don't need to decide right this minute," Jeff said. "Go home and think about it. Give me a call when you've made up your mind."

"All right," Paul said. "I'll give you a call later this afternoon."

"That's good," Jeff said. "If I should decide to send you, I'll probably want you to fly out there first thing in the morning."

Jeff Owensford placed a call to Paul later in the afternoon.

"Paul, have you come to a decision?" Jeff asked. He didn't for one minute think that Paul would have enough guts to turn him down.

"Yes, I've decided to help you," Paul said. "It isn't because of the money. It's to make sure that Emilia Wright is not harmed. This will definitely be the last assignment before I retire. Is that agreeable to you?"

"Absolutely," Jeff said. "You've got my word on it."

"Then I'll call and make a reservation for an early flight tomorrow morning." Paul said. "I'll go directly to the boat and check things out before I call you."

"Fine," Jeff said. "I'll be waiting for your call."

After Jeff hung up, he wondered if maybe he should go there too. But first he wanted to call the doctor in the morning about his test results. He wasn't getting any headaches since he started taking the capsules the doctor prescribed, which he thought was a good sign. He figured he could decide about going to the Cape after he talked to the doctor.

~ NINETEEN ~

As Emilia watched the noon news, she felt numb and it was almost as though they were describing some incident which happened to someone else. She realized her situation was perilous and could become even more so depending upon Bill's condition. She had no qualms about her kidnappers, whose names she now knew were Jake and Carl. She knew they would sacrifice her in an instant to protect themselves. Even now, as she watched Jake pace back and forth, she sensed that he was extremely agitated by the news that Bill Stewart was in critical condition.

Emilia said a silent prayer that Bill would pull through. Even though she realized it was his job to protect her, she still felt a sense of responsibility for what happened to him.

"We didn't mean for anyone to get hurt that way," Jake said. "We just wanted to make sure they were out of commission and wouldn't be able to follow us."

"I know," Emilia said. "I don't think you would deliberately try to kill someone." *I will say whatever I think you want to hear and gain the advantage of being in your good graces, providing you have any,* she thought.

Emilia decided to try another approach with Jake.

"How much are you being paid to keep me here?" she asked. "Perhaps I could arrange to pay you much more to let me go."

"It's not a matter of how much we're getting paid to keep you here," Jake said. "Your abduction is just one of many assignments we get from our boss. Besides always having work, we don't have to worry if we're caught. The organization he works for gives us legal protection if we are caught, and they make sure we get off. I don't even have to think about your offer. For one thing, how far do you think we'd get before they would deliver their own brand of retaliation?"

Emilia knew the organization Jake referred to was the APLA. A chill ran through her when she realized the extent of their evil activities. It reminded her of stories told about various mobs, consisting of cold-blooded gangsters, living in Chicago many years ago. This was much worse and was nationwide as well.

"With the kind of money I'm talking about, you could go where they will never find you," she said. "At least think about it."

"Would you like a sandwich?" Jake asked. "I'm going to call Carl for lunch."

"Yes, thank you." She replied. Emilia sensed that was the end of her attempted bribery.

Emilia just started to eat when Carl came down to the cabin. He was still trying to catch fish for dinner. Emilia wondered how he could be so engrossed in fishing, considering the circumstances surrounding the events of this morning. But then she remembered her initial thought that Carl did not appear too bright. Maybe I should try to work on him she thought.

Right now, the recent experience of her panic attack was too fresh in her mind to contemplate any risk.

After lunch, Emilia was left below in the cabin and told to clean up while Jake and Carl went up on deck. She was so glad to be alone, she didn't even mind washing the dishes. She heard Jake talking to Carl when he opened the door and came back down about an hour later to check on her. Every time the door at the top of the steps opened, Emilia took a deep breath of the fresh air that drifted down into the cabin.

Emilia watched as Jake went to the refrigerator for a can of soda and then came and sat down at the table with her.

"Do you know how to make fish?" he asked. "That is if Carl is able to catch any."

"Yes, I know how to fry or bake it," Emilia said. "Nothing fancy though." She got up and walked to the sink for a glass of water.

"Do you think I might go up on deck sometime to get some fresh air?" she asked. "It's so stuffy down here and that musty smell is getting to me."

"That musty smell is from the boat being closed up for so long," Jake said. "Maybe I'll take you up on deck for a while after dark. You can't go up in the daylight because someone might recognize you. Besides, I can't be sure you won't call out for help if anyone comes within hearing distance."

"I told you I won't try to get away," Emilia said. She watched as Jake finished his soda and tossed the can into the trash. She noticed he looked at her like what he said next would be the end of the discussion.

"You might not do it intentionally," he said. "It would be automatic if you got the chance. I'm not willing to risk it, so you just do as you're told."

Emilia decided to drop it. She already got him to say he might take her up on deck after dark. She didn't want to push it and lose that too. She wondered how long they planned to keep her there. Maybe Jake doesn't know she thought.

"When will you find out how long we have to stay here?" she asked.

"We'll be here until they move us to another location, or they decide to let you go," Jake said. "I don't make the decisions. I just follow orders."

Emilia sensed that Jake was becoming annoyed at her questions. She watched him as he got up and walked over to the magazine rack beside the chair to look for something to read. She decided to ask one more.

"And who gives the orders?" she asked. "Or is that privileged information?"

"It is for you," Jake said. "I'm going back up on deck for a while. Why don't you watch TV and try to relax." She watched him go up the steps to the door.

Emilia was again left alone to contemplate her fate. She tried to control her imagination, which conjured up the worst possible scenarios and played havoc with her emotions. She wondered what they planned to do with her. Perhaps she would be tied up and left to die. Her heart raced at the thought. No one knew where she was. How would Dennis ever find her? She felt the tears sting her eyes as she thought of him.

The idea that she might have to spend days or even weeks in this cabin was beyond her immediate comprehension. It felt like she'd been here for days, when in reality it was only four or five hours at the most. She didn't know if she could cope with this situation for any extended period of time. Emilia walked over and turned on the TV. Maybe Jake was right she thought. She should try to relax.

About twenty minutes later, Emilia heard someone coming down the steps. She looked up and saw Carl carrying two fish he'd just caught.

"Jake said you would cook the fish for us," he said. "What time do you think you'll be making them? I'm used to eating around 4:30."

"I guess I can have them ready at 4:30," Emilia said. "Where is Jake?"

"He went to use the phone and pick up some groceries," Carl replied. "He should be back in time to eat. I told him to bring some french fries to go with the fish. I'm supposed to watch you and make sure you don't leave the cabin." Emilia noticed he smiled as though he was pleased to have this responsibility.

"I won't try to leave the cabin," Emilia said. "Who did Jake have to call?" She thought she might trick Carl into telling her something.

"I don't know," he said. "You're awfully pretty, you know that?"

"Thank you," Emilia said. "Do you want to help me make the fish?"

Suddenly, Emilia was frightened and wondered if she could distract Carl away from the attention he was now focusing on her. She saw Carl's gaze move from her face to her chest. Her face grew hot as his gaze continued downward. She felt the knot in her stomach tighten as he slowly undressed her with his eyes. She knew what was on his mind. She realized she would not have the strength to defend herself if he began to make physical advances toward her. She must find some way to keep him occupied and divert his attention away from her. She pulled herself together and, pretending not to notice the lewd look in his eyes, walked around to the other side of the table and started cleaning the fish.

"Would you like to help me with this?" Emilia asked. "I'll teach you how to make really good fried fish." She quickly looked at his face to see if he appeared distracted. "Would you please heat up the grease for me?" She sighed with relief when Carl walked over to the cupboard to get the oil. She had succeeded in diverting Carl's brief attention span to the art of cooking fish. Now, if I can only keep him busy until Jake comes back she thought.

It seemed like an eternity before Emilia heard Jake's footsteps on the deck. She went limp with relief when she saw him come down the steps with the groceries. She knew she had a close call. She also knew Jake sensed something was wrong when he came into the cabin.

"What's been going on?" Jake asked.

"Nothing," Carl replied. "I was just helping her cook the fish." Jake then turned and looked at Emilia.

"What did Carl do?" Jake asked. "You look scared to death."

"He didn't do anything," Emilia said. "It was what I thought he was going to do that scared me." Emilia knew Jake understood exactly what she meant. He walked over and stood directly in front of Carl.

"I'm telling you right now," Jake said. "If you so much as touch her, I'll see that you're back working in that bar where I found you. Now go watch TV until dinner is ready."

After dinner, Emilia watched TV while Jake and Carl went up on deck. She couldn't wait for it to get dark so she could go on deck and get some fresh air. Even though she heard Jake say the boat was supposed to be mechanically sound, she realized the musty odor that permeated the cabin undoubtedly resulted from years of neglect. She knew by the thick layer of dust that the boat wasn't used for quite a few years. She examined all the drawers to see if she could find out who owned the boat but came up empty handed. Someone did a very thorough job of eliminating any identifying characteristics. Emilia hoped Jake would remember his promise to let her go up on deck when it got dark.

Emilia wondered where they were going to sleep. There were only two bunks in the cabin. She didn't even have a clean change of clothes. There was no way she was going to undress to wash her clothes out. The bathroom was barely big enough to turn around in. This is no luxury liner she thought.

Emilia wondered who was responsible for placing her in this precarious situation. She wished she had them here right now. She was so angry at being held against her will that she suddenly felt a hot flush surge through her entire body like a fire. She wondered if she were going to have a stroke. She finally understood how one develops a feeling of malice toward another, and it wasn't a welcome emotion.

After the sun set, Emilia heard Jake call down that she could come up on deck for some air. Emilia ran up the steps and onto the deck. She walked over to the railing and watched the last of the sunset. She could feel the chill in the air, which she knew follows the sunset when you're near the ocean, but it felt wonderful. She didn't want to waste a precious moment of outdoor liberation and she savored every breath of fresh air. She closed her eyes and tried to forget where she was as the ocean breeze caressed her cheeks. Just then, she heard Jake walk up beside her.

"Thanks," Emilia said. "I appreciate your letting me out for some air."

"I've got to keep you healthy," he said. "Why don't you walk around the deck and get a little exercise."

"That's a good idea," Emilia said. It will relieve some stress she thought. She wanted to remain as active as possible in case she needed extra stamina during the course of this ordeal. Who knows what might be required before this nightmare is over she thought?

Emilia stayed up on deck with Jake as guard until eleven o'clock. She was sorry to hear him say that it was time to go in. For some reason, she felt safer outside and in the dark but she knew better than to argue. When they entered the cabin, Emilia saw that Carl had fallen asleep in front of the TV.

"You can have whichever bunk you'd like," Jake said. "I'll take the other one and Carl will sleep on deck with one eye open." Jake walked over to the chair and shook Carl awake. She heard Carl groan when Jake told him to go up on deck and keep watch during the night. At least she didn't have to worry about Carl attacking her as she slept.

Emilia chose the lower bunk. Without undressing, she lay down and covered with a blanket she found at the bottom of the bed. In a way, she was thankful for each opportunity that allowed her to just close her eyes and try to forget where she was. She said a few silent prayers, especially for Bill Stewart, before she drifted off to sleep.

Emilia woke up to the aroma of coffee brewing. She looked over and saw that Jake was cooking what smelled like bacon and eggs. She yawned as she sat up on the side of the bunk bed and stretched to get rid of the kinks. She couldn't recall ever sleeping on a harder mattress.

She was still there on the bed when she heard voices from above. Jake started up the steps just as the door opened. Emilia was astonished when she saw Paul Freedman, whom she met at the school board meeting, come down the steps with Carl. She knew he hadn't seen her yet. It was quite obvious to Emilia that he knew Jake and Carl and she realized that her two kidnappers must work for Paul Freedman.

"I'm just making breakfast," Jake said. "Would you like something?"

"No, thanks," Paul replied. "I've already eaten. I will have a cup of coffee if you're making some." Emilia saw him look her way and she knew he saw the unbelief in her eyes. She watched him cringe from the accusing look she shot his way.

"Are you all right," Paul asked. "They haven't hurt you, have they?"

"Does it really matter?" Emilia asked. "It's obvious to me that you don't care one way or the other. If you did, you wouldn't be involved in this." She couldn't hold back the icy tone she used on him. He walked over and looked down at her.

"I do care, whether you believe it or not," Paul said. "That's the only reason I agreed to come here. It's to make sure they don't hurt you. My wish would be total abstinence from the entire situation. If you knew the whole story, you'd realize I really don't have any choice if I ever want to be able to live with myself."

Emilia somehow sensed the sincerity in what he'd said and she remembered how she once judged Brad before she knew the facts. At least she felt his intention was to make sure she wouldn't be hurt and she was ready to accept anyone on that basis.

"I believe I know now why I thought I'd met you before," Emilia said. "You bear a striking resemblance to an uncle of mine, Andrew O'Brien, who disappeared many years ago before I was born. When I got home from the school board meeting, I looked through my old photographs and found a picture of him. He was in a picture with my grandmother Emma, along with my mother, Katherine, and my Uncle James." Emilia noticed the same flicker of recognition in Paul Freedman's eyes that she'd noticed when they met. Hearing the names must have triggered it she thought.

"We'll talk about this later," he whispered to Emilia. She watched as he walked back over to talk to Jake.

Emilia realized Paul was visibly shaken when she mentioned the photograph and knew there must be some connection for him. Perhaps after breakfast, they would find themselves alone and be able to discuss it again.

"While you three are eating, I'm going to walk down to the end of the marina and make a phone call," Paul said. "Is there anything you need while I'm out?"

"No," Jake said. "I think when you come back Carl and I should go to the larger chain store for our groceries. That little mom and pop store at the end of the marina charges an arm and a leg for everything. That's if it's OK with you."

"Sure thing," Paul said. "I should be back in about fifteen minutes."

Emilia realized as soon as he came back, they would get their chance to talk alone with Jake and Carl out of the way. Emilia wondered how much information Paul would share with her.

Emilia sat down at the table with Jake and Carl to eat breakfast. She watched as Paul Freedman went back up the steps and she listened to his footsteps overhead as he walked across the deck. She wondered why he left so quickly to use the phone. It was probably to report to the person responsible for her being here. She tried to imagine what type of twisted individual could issue an order to have someone kidnapped. He would have to be vicious and unfeeling she thought as she sipped her coffee. She felt sure she didn't know anyone like that.

Emilia finished her breakfast and was clearing the table when she heard Paul return. She thought he appeared anxious and wondered if it had to do with the phone call. She sensed he was eager to get rid of Jake and Carl.

"You and Carl can go whenever you like," Paul said to Jake. "Take your time. You could probably use a break. Maybe Miss Wright and I will play a game of chess while you're gone. Do you play, Miss Wright?"

"Not too well," she replied. "But at least it will help to pass the time." Emilia heard Jake quickly take Paul up on his offer.

"Thanks," Jake said. "We could use a break away from this boat. We'll get a little exercise and then stop for the groceries on the way back. We won't be long."

After Jake and Carl left, Emilia sat down at the table with Paul and poured them a cup of coffee. She was not surprised when Paul asked her to tell him all she knew about the people in the photograph that she mentioned when he first arrived. So, she was right. There was a flicker of recognition when he heard the names.

"Actually, I really only knew two of the people in the picture," Emilia said. "My mother, whose name was Katherine, and my Uncle Jim, who died when I was about five years old."

"What about the other two," Paul asked. "What do you remember hearing about them?"

"My Uncle Andrew disappeared without a trace," Emilia said. "My Grandmother Emma apparently died unexpectedly about two weeks later." Emilia took a sip of coffee while she waited for Paul Freedman to respond.

"Did they search for your Uncle Andrew?" Paul asked.

"Yes, they did," Emilia said. "My grandmother hired a detective who thought he may have gone to Chicago. But she couldn't afford to retain the detective." Emilia waited as Paul concentrated on what she said.

"So this Andrew was never heard of again?" Paul asked.

"No, he wasn't," Emilia said. "Then, according to my mother, my grandmother died about two weeks later."

"What was the cause of your grandmother's death?" Paul asked. "Or didn't you ever hear?"

"She had a chronic heart condition," Emilia said.

"What was your grandmother's name again?" Paul asked.

"It was Emma O'Brien," Emilia said. "My uncle who disappeared was Andrew O'Brien. Does any of this mean anything to you?"

"There's something about the names," Paul said. "I've got to concentrate on them and see if I can remember." Emilia could see how intense Paul was in his effort to remember. She wished she could help him in some way.

"I don't understand what it is you're trying to remember," Emilia said. "Do you think you might be related to them?"

"Emilia, I've been suffering from amnesia for approximately forty-three years," Paul said. "I was found wandering the streets of Chicago near death from a beating I'd sustained. I recovered physically but was left with amnesia."

"Then it's possible that you are my Uncle Andrew," Emilia exclaimed. "The time element is exactly right. Who was it that found you? Didn't they have any information to help determine your identity?" Emilia was excited as the realization hit home that this Paul Freedman might be her Uncle Andrew.

"It was Jeff Owensford," Paul said. "If I am Andrew O'Brien, he would have known." Emilia watched the hurt look on Paul's face turn to one of anger.

"I don't understand," she said. "How is that possible? Why would he do such a thing?" She was completely bewildered.

"I don't know," Paul said. "Please don't say anything in front of Jake or Carl. If you're right, neither one of us will be safe if Jeff thinks I've discovered what he's kept from me all these years. The whole thing defies reason or logic." Emilia could see that Paul Freedman was as baffled as she was.

"Let's assume you are Andrew O'Brien," Emilia said. "Then Jeff might have been responsible for your beating."

"Why do you suppose Andrew went to Chicago?" Paul asked.

"I have no idea," Emilia said.

"Do you recall hearing of anything out of the ordinary before his disappearance? Any family problems or any altercations with anyone?"

"Nothing like that, except for my mother's pregnancy," Emilia said.

"Tell me about that," Paul said. "It might have some bearing on this."

Emilia poured them another cup of coffee. Then she sat down and told Paul what happened up to when she found out that Brad was her biological father. She was aware that Paul paid close attention, particularly when she told of the bitterness Jeff Owensford felt toward Brad Owensford to this day. As she told Paul about them, it suddenly dawned on her that Andrew O'Brien might have followed Jeff Owensford to

Chicago to confront him for deliberately causing the breakup of his sister and Brad. She asked Paul what he thought and he agreed it was very possible. Emilia drank her coffee while she waited for Paul to absorb all she'd told him.

"You would think Brad would hate Jeff, rather than the other way around," Paul said. Emilia sensed that Paul Freedman was surprised to hear what Jeff had done.

"On the contrary, when their father disinherited Jeff, Brad made sure he received enough money to live comfortably for the rest of his life," Emilia said.

"That's incredible, considering how he messed up Brad's life," Paul said.

"Why did you say that Jeff hates Brad?" Emilia asked. "I know the two of them don't get along very well, but hates a pretty strong word."

"What would you think if I told you Jeff Owensford is behind your abduction?" Paul asked.

"I'd find it awfully hard to believe that my own uncle would expose me to the likes of Jake and Carl," she replied. "Not to mention what he'd be putting Brad through. But what purpose would he have for doing such a thing?"

"I believe he plans to call Brad," Paul said. "He intends to make a demand for an unprecedented amount of money to be delivered into the hands of the APLA. He's grown tired of getting the extortion money in dribbles by threats of harm to Katherine, and now you."

Emilia felt shock go through her like she'd been hit with a live wire as she listened to Paul's explanation of the ongoing extortion against Brad. She didn't know whether to believe Paul as he, too, was involved in this whole mess. But if her assumption that he might be Andrew O'Brien is right, then Paul Freedman is also one of Jeff's victims she thought.

"What does Jeff have to do with the APLA," Emilia asked.

"I believe he is a silent executive officer in the organization," Paul said. "His investment brokerage firm is just a convenient front to hide his affiliation with them."

Emilia felt the heat course through her entire body, from the top of her head to her feet. Her hands trembled and her eyes filled up with tears of righteous anger. "What can we do to stop this from happening?" Emilia asked. "We can't allow them to get their hands on Brad's money, which they will then use to undermine our own government. There must be something awfully wrong with Jeff Owensford. I find his actions despicable."

"I'm beginning to think you're right," Paul said. "I'm going up on deck and see if the relaxation techniques they taught me in the hospital might help me remember."

Emilia wished again there were some way she could help Paul to remember. As she watched him start up the steps, she heard him say, "Whatever you do, don't let Jake or Carl know what we've discussed."

"Wait," Emilia called. "Do you think we'll be able to get away from them?" Emilia noticed he had a tender look in his eye when he turned to answer her. And suddenly she saw the resemblance to her mother. There was little doubt he was her uncle. She impulsively ran over and hugged him. She felt him respond with tenderness.

"I'll try to come up with some plan," Paul said. Emilia sensed how serious he was as he continued. "Don't for one minute underestimate the danger. They can be ruthless, especially Carl. I'm going up on deck now so they don't think we're getting along too well and become suspicious. I'll have to be particularly careful when I make my phone call to Jeff after dinner. We may think he's vicious and evil, but he's not stupid. Over the years, I've noticed he seems to have this uncanny sense of intuition about what people are really thinking." So that's where I get it, Emilia thought as she watched Paul go up the steps.

Emilia prayed that Paul would regain his memory. She found it inconceivable that Jeff arranged for the beating that almost killed him. Worse yet, that he allowed Paul to believe he was obligated to him for saving his life. What a monster Jeff Owensford must be she thought. She hoped that if Paul remembered the circumstances behind his amnesia, he could keep his emotions in check until they were safely away.

Emilia realized she never fully appreciated her freedom until it was taken from her. That's the way most Americans must be she thought. Otherwise, they wouldn't risk their freedom by allowing the APLA to remain in existence.

- TWENTY -

Jeff walked into the doctor's office about eight o'clock. When he telephoned early this morning, the nurse told him Dr. Scott wanted to see him and asked if he could come in.

Jeff assumed the doctor wanted to see him with regard to his test results and he wondered what they revealed. There's no use going off the deep end and anticipating the worst just because he wants to see you he thought. I've got to remain calm. Doctors are known to be alarmists and it's probably nothing serious. In any case, I'll be talking to him very shortly.

Jeff was visibly nervous. He turned the pages of a magazine unconsciously, without even realizing the content, as he waited to be called in to see the doctor. Finally, the nurse called his name.

Doctor Scott's facial expression gave no indication of whether this was serious or not as he came into the examining room. He sat down to finish looking over Jeff's chart before he turned to address him.

"Jeff, you can relax," Dr. Scott said. "Your tests didn't reveal anything physically abnormal."

"Then why did you want to see me," Jeff asked. "I was quite concerned when your nurse called and asked me to come in."

"It's because of those severe headaches and memory relapses you've been experiencing," Dr. Scott said. "The memory lapses could be potentially dangerous, especially if you happen to be driving your car or operating any type of machinery. I don't think they're due entirely to your headaches. I think the pain associated with your headache becomes so severe that you black out. What we need to do is find out what's causing the headaches. They could even be psychosomatic."

"How do we determine that?" Jeff asked. "I told you I don't know why I get them."

"They could be stress related," Dr. Scott said. "The MRI test indicated nothing physical that would cause them. Perhaps your headaches are the result of some mental pressure you're under. It wouldn't hurt to get a psychiatric evaluation. It could be any number of things, even depression."

"I don't need a psychiatrist," Jeff said. "There's nothing wrong with my mind."

"We don't always recognize how our mental health can affect our bodies," Dr. Scott said. "There's no stigma attached to having a mental evaluation done."

Jeff was angry and he felt himself losing control. He sensed that Dr. Scott also recognized this and it reaffirmed his suspicion that Jeff's problem might be mental rather than physical.

"Isn't there anyone you could take into your confidence and discuss this with?" Dr. Scott asked. "Perhaps some family member who might have noticed a personality change in you."

"I'm afraid that's out of the question," Jeff said. "There's absolutely no one I can trust. They would like to see me put away so they can get their hands on my money. They think I don't know, but I've heard them plotting against me, even my own daughter and my grandchildren. They all hate me. But I'll show them someday when I come into power. I will be invincible then, and everyone will be obliged to do my will."

Jeff noticed the way Dr. Scott was looking at him and he struggled to pull himself together but could not. He was aware that Dr. Scott watched him as he continued on with his tirade of extreme agitation. Jeff knew from experience he would either collapse or change to a euphoric state. When the blackness began to close in, Jeff heard Dr. Scott ask his nurse to retrieve the name of Jeff's closest relative from the file.

When Jeff came to, he opened his eyes and saw Dr. Scott looking down at him and listened to what he was saying.

"Jeff, listen to me carefully," he said. "You were speaking in an unbalanced way before you passed out. There is no longer any doubt in my mind that you need psychiatric help. Please believe me, it is possible you may even harm someone if you don't get medication to help you."

"I'll think about it," Jeff said. "I'll call and let you know."

He had no intention of following the doctor's advice. Just because he'd had a few spells didn't mean that he was crazy. Dr. Scott probably owns stock in some insane asylum he thought as he hurried from his office and headed back home.

Jeff heard the phone ring as he opened the door and he ran to answer it.

"Jeff, it's me," Paul said. "I went to the boat and everything is under control. I left the three of them to eat breakfast, and I'm going to let Jake and Carl go to the store when I get back."

"Aren't you afraid Emilia might try to escape?" Jeff asked. He couldn't quite picture Paul restraining anyone all alone.

"No, I'm not," Paul replied. "She has some sort of phobia about being held down and not being able to move. Jake said she told him it was some sort of panic disorder and she's filled with dread at the very idea of being tied up again. I don't think she will take the risk."

"Do you think it's safe to stay put?" Jeff asked. "Or should we move her to some other location?"

"I think it's safe for right now," Paul replied. "By the way, I was followed all the way to Sandwich. If I hadn't stopped at a diner to eat, I would never have noticed. I managed to slip out the back way and hail a cab to take me to the marina."

"Are you quite sure you weren't followed?" Jeff asked. He wondered why anyone would be following Paul. Perhaps Paul's imagination is working overtime, Jeff thought. Either that or it's because he works for me.

"Yes, I'm positive," Paul replied. "I even had the driver pass the diner to make sure their car was still in the parking area." Jeff was amazed to hear that Paul used his brains for once.

"Give me a call later on," Jeff said. "I may decide to come out there myself."

- *TWENTY-ONE* -

Chief Archer and Agent Lawson arrived at Brad Owensford's house about eight-thirty in the morning. Dennis looked up as Brad's housekeeper showed them out to the back deck where he and Brad were having coffee.

"Would you like some coffee?" Dennis asked. "There are extra cups on the table. Just help yourself."

"Thanks," Agent Lawson said. "I hope we're not interrupting your breakfast."

"Not at all," Brad said. "We just finished a few minutes ago and came out here to watch the ocean while we had our coffee." Dennis could see that Brad was worried about why they were there.

"I'm afraid I've come to give you some rather startling news," Agent Lawson said. "I'm sure it will be quite hard for you to accept and believe." Dennis realized Agent Lawson was talking about Jeff Owensford but he sensed that Brad thought he was about to hear bad news about Emilia.

"Is it about Emilia?" Brad asked. Dennis could hear how alarmed he was.

"No, it's not," Agent Lawson said. "I'm sorry, I should have told you it wasn't before I started. I realize how worried you must be about Emilia."

"Then what is it about?" Brad asked. "Right now, I don't care about anything but finding Emilia."

"In a way, it does concern Emilia," Dennis said. "Please listen to what Agent Lawson has to tell you."

"This is about Jeff Owensford," Agent Lawson said. "You're not going to like hearing it anymore than I like telling you. There's no use beating around the bush. Your brother, Jeff Owensford, is responsible for Emilia's abduction." Dennis saw the look of denial on Brad's face as soon as Agent Lawson finished talking.

"You must be crazy," Brad said. "I know Jeff and I don't get along, but what reason would he have to do something like this to me?" Dennis could hear the excitement in Brad's voice as Agent Lawson continued.

"The same reason he's been doing it to you for the last forty years," Agent Lawson said. "Aside from his blatant hatred for you, he wants your money to support the APLA." Dennis saw Brad look at him for his reaction.

"I'm afraid what he's telling you is true," Dennis said.

"What has he to do with that organization?" Brad asked. "You must be mistaken." Dennis had already warned them Brad would not believe them.

"No, I'm sorry to say we're not," Agent Lawson said. "Jeff has been an inactive executive officer in that organization almost from its very inception."

"I don't know what to say," Brad said. "You're right, I can't believe that of Jeff."

"There's more," Dennis said. "We have reason to believe that a Mr. Paul Freedman, who's been working for Jeff for just as many years, is really Andrew O'Brien, Emilia's uncle who disappeared many years ago."

"But why would he have gone to Chicago to work for Jeff," Brad asked.

"We don't think he did," Dennis said. "We believe he went to Chicago to avenge his sister, Katherine, for the trouble Jeff caused her by his deliberate deception. You see, Paul Freedman suffers from amnesia. All he can remember is that Jeff found him wandering the streets of Chicago close to death from a beating he sustained. He recovered physically, but he was left with amnesia. The hospital gave him the name of Paul Freedman, and Jeff has exercised control over Paul all these years by instilling in him a sense of obligation for saving his life. In reality, we believe that

Jeff ordered Paul killed, and they bungled the job, which meant Jeff had to keep tabs on Paul to make sure he never remembered who he really was."

"You're making Jeff out to be some sort of monster," Brad said. "He would have to be evil and vicious to do the things you're accusing him of."

"Perhaps he is," Dennis said. "This morning, Agent Lawson's men followed Paul Freedman all the way from Chicago to Sandwich before they lost him. We have reason to believe Jeff may have sent him to oversee Emilia, wherever it is they are keeping her. Can you think of anywhere near Sandwich where they might have taken her?"

"No, I really can't offhand," Brad replied.

"I think Emilia might already suspect who Paul Freedman is," Dennis said. "That would explain the photograph you found in her handbag. Suppose he should remember everything when he sees her and talks to her? She does resemble Katherine quite a bit. That alone might jog Paul's memory."

"Then, unless he keeps his head, they might both be in big trouble," Agent Lawson said. "We've already come to the conclusion that if Jeff believes Paul is regaining his memory, he would be signing his own death warrant."

"What can we do?" Brad asked. "Do you want me to call and confront Jeff?"

"No, I think that's the last thing the FBI wants," Dennis said.

"That's right," Agent Lawson said. "Eventually, we think he will call you and make some outrageous demand. But, until he does, we will use the time to continue our search for Emilia, and hope that we find her before Jeff calls."

"In the meantime, Brad might think of some place Jeff might have taken her," Dennis said.

"I'll do the best I can," Brad said.

"Give us a call if you come up with anything," Chief Archer said as he and Agent Lawson got up to go.

"I'll walk out with you," Dennis said. "I'm going to my office and then I thought I'd stop at the library and see what kind of information I can dig up on the APLA. I might find something we can use. I'll be back later," Dennis said to Brad as they went into the house.

When Dennis returned home, Brad filled him in on a call he got from Joyce. Dennis was surprised to hear that Jeff's doctor called Joyce and asked her to try and persuade her father to have a psychiatric evaluation. Dr. Scott indicated he thought Jeff's migraine headaches might stem from some form of mental disorder.

"What did you tell her?" Dennis asked.

"I didn't have the heart to tell her what we've already found out about Jeff," Brad replied. "She's worried enough as it is."

"Then his atrocious actions over the years are, in all probability, attributable to a mental condition," Dennis said.

"I should have suspected as much," Brad said. "Even when we were younger, Jeff was considered a maverick, and seemed to prefer being alone in his own little world. I'm sorry now I didn't pay more attention to his unusual behavior. Perhaps if he had gotten the help then, he would be all right now."

"You can't blame yourself," Dennis said. "Obviously, your parents weren't concerned or they would have seen that he received professional help. Maybe we should let Agent Lawson and Chief Archer know about this."

Brad agreed and Dennis put through a call to Chief Archer who was out of the office. He then tried Agent Lawson who was in. Dennis told him about Brad's call from Joyce Hanson, Jeff Owensford's daughter.

"From what the doctor told Joyce," Dennis said. "Jeff could pose a danger to himself as well as others. He feels Jeff should be put on medication as soon as possible."

"I agree," Agent Lawson said. "I hope his daughter is able to convince him."

"I'm afraid the danger the doctor referred to might be to Emilia," Dennis said. "I just don't want to take that risk."

"Let's wait and see what happens," Agent Lawson said. "At least until tomorrow. What do you think?"

"I agree," Dennis said. "Another day can't make that much difference in his condition. It will give us more time to search for Emilia. I wonder if Paul Freedman is with them now? He must have been heading for their hideout when we lost him. Maybe being in close contact with Emilia will jog his memory."

"That would be good for Emilia," Agent Lawson said. "But dangerous for Paul Freedman."

"Only if they think he's regained his memory," Dennis said. "If he does and can hide it from them, he might help Emilia escape."

"That's possible," Agent Lawson said. "If we can get Emilia back, and if Paul has pertinent information, and is willing to testify against Jeff, we might be able to wind this case up."

"I think we're going to need a little more than Paul Freedman will be able to provide," Dennis said. "In any case, it will be the end of the financial support for the APLA, and hopefully, put them completely out of business. Of course, it will take many years to undo the damage they've already done.

"It's just mind boggling," Agent Lawson said. "To comprehend how the people of this nation have allowed an obscure organization, historically known to be initiated by the Communist Party, to become instrumental in actually changing and establishing new guidelines for policy in all the diversified branches of our government.

"At least, we now have the chance to stop them before it's too late," Dennis said.

After he hung up, he tried Chief Archer again and waited impatiently for him to come to the phone. He was calling to tell him Brad remembered that Jeff owned a large cabin cruiser many years ago. Brad didn't know if he still had it, but there was a possibility he did and Emilia might be on it. It seemed an eternity before Chief Archer got on the phone.

"Dennis," he said. "What's up?"

Dennis relayed what Brad had remembered and Chief Archer asked if Brad knew where Jeff kept the boat?

"No, he doesn't," Dennis said. "It was a long time ago."

"Well, it's the only lead we have," Chief Archer said. "We can run it through the computer to see if there's a registration for one in Jeff Owensford's name."

"If there is, we'll have to find out where the boat is docked," Dennis said. "Do you realize how many marinas are on the Cape?"

"I sure do," Chief Archer said. "It might take quite a while to locate it."

"Perhaps Agent Lawson could help," Dennis said. "They could put some people on it too. I think we should divide it up by area and start with the closest to where she was kidnapped and work outward."

"That makes sense," Chief Archer said. "But first let's make sure there is a boat registration in Jeff Owensford's name. If there is, I'll give Agent Lawson a call right away. I'll get back to you."

"I think I'll come over to the station to help," Dennis said. "First, I'll ask Brad to call Joyce Hanson to see if she might know something about Jeff's boat. I'll see you shortly."

Dennis waited and listened while Brad called Joyce to see if she knew anything about Jeff's boat. Dennis noticed Brad look at him and shake his head no as he continued to talk to Joyce. Dennis waved he was leaving and left Brad to talk to Joyce.

When Dennis got to the police station, he saw that Agent Lawson was already there talking to Chief Archer. Dennis heard Agent Lawson tell him that they received word that Jeff Owensford left Chicago in a private plane with a logged destination of Hyannis Airport. When Agent Lawson finally got through to security at the airport, he was advised the plane landed about thirty minutes before he called. Jeff Owensford had already left the airport.

"Do you realize what that means?" Dennis asked. "It means that Emilia is alone with Jeff Owensford, Paul Freedman and the two who kidnapped her."

"Take it easy," Agent Lawson said. "I don't think Miss Wright is in any immediate danger. We're almost certain they took her in order to get to Brad Owensford. I expect he will soon be receiving a call from them."

"How about the boat registration?" Dennis asked. "Does Jeff still own a boat?"

"We ran the recent boat registrations through the computer," Chief Archer said. "There is a large boat registered in Jeff Owensford's name. I've already assigned several detectives to check the various marinas in the area. As soon as we locate the boat, we can make our move."

~ *TWENTY-TWO* ~

Emilia heard footsteps and then voices shortly after Paul went up on deck and realized Jake and Carl had returned. She heard Paul ask if they brought him a paper. Jake told him he'd bring it up to him as soon as he took the groceries down to the cabin. She heard Jake ask Paul if Emilia gave him any trouble while they were gone. If Jake only knew she thought.

Emilia was watching TV when Jake and Carl came down with the groceries.

"That looks like "Arsenic and Old Lace" with Cary Grant," Carl said. "That's one of my favorites."

"Yes, it is," Emilia said. "Do you like to watch old movies?"

"I sure do," Carl replied. "Which is your favorite?"

"Oh, I like so many," Emilia said. "I guess maybe it would be "Random Harvest."

"I don't think I've ever seen that one," Carl said. "Who plays the lead?"

"Ronald Coleman and Greer Garson," Emilia replied. "You must make sure you see it if it's ever on again."

"I'll look for it," Carl said. Emilia got up and went over to the table when Carl came over and sat down next to her. She decided to humor him whenever possible but she couldn't stand being near him. He actually gave her the creeps.

Carl didn't sit there too long before Emilia heard Jake tell him to go up on deck and keep his eyes open. Emilia noticed Jake handed Carl the newspaper and told him to take it up to Paul. She started to make lunch while Jake put the groceries away.

Emilia found an opportunity to talk to Paul alone shortly after lunch when Jake and Carl went on deck to fish. Paul came down to the cabin and joined Emilia at the table.

"Were you able to remember anything?" she asked.

"I remember a great deal," Paul said. "I am Andrew O'Brien, your uncle. I began thinking of Katherine and all of a sudden I could see her with her small button nose and radiant smile. Then I remembered my mother and my brother James."

Emilia heard the catch in his voice when he spoke of losing his mother even though it happened many years ago. To Paul, it might just as well have happened yesterday. "I'm sorry," she said. "I know how you feel. What else do you remember?"

"I remember the old neighborhood, the school, my friends. I also remember Brad and Jeff Owensford and Robert Wright."

"You were able to recall quite a lot," Emilia said.

"Yes, and I also remember how furious I was with Jeff for the way he manipulated Brad and Katherine. He robbed them of their chance for happiness. I know I went looking for him but that part still eludes me."

"I'm sure it will all come back in time," Emilia said. "Will you be able to hide this from Jeff?"

"It's going to be hard," Paul said. "I know now that Jeff tried to have me killed and, only by the grace of God, failed. At least, I'll only have to talk to him on the phone and not face to face. I can do it if I don't have to look him in the eye."

Emilia suddenly felt a strong kinship to Paul. He was, after all, her uncle. She knew she and Paul must somehow get away and try to reach Dennis. Emilia suggested the best chance would be after dark when she was allowed on deck.

"I saw a dinghy hanging from the side of the boat," she said.

"We could lower the dinghy into the water and try to make our way along the canal and out to the Bay," Paul suggested.

Emilia agreed. "If they discover we're gone, they will more than likely think we left the boat and headed for the phone booth at the end of the marina. After that, they will probably get in their car and scour the immediate neighborhood. I don't think they will look for us in the water." At least not until they've exhausted every other avenue she thought.

"I don't either," Paul said.

"Once we get out to the Bay, we'll row along the shore until we get near the preserve," she said. "Then we'll go ashore and walk down the beach from there. We will eventually come to Brad's house."

"What did Jake buy for dinner?" Paul asked. "I hope it was something heavy and filling."

"I get it," Emilia said. "You hope they stuff themselves and doze off so we'll get a good head start. I'll see what I can whip up. You don't mind if I give you another hug, do you?"

"Anytime," he said. "As long as Jake and Carl don't see you."

"I guess you better go up on deck before they get suspicious," Emilia said. "Maybe we'll get our chance tonight after dinner when it's dark."

As soon as Paul went up on deck, Emilia started dinner. She had everything she needed to make spaghetti and meatballs. Off hand, she couldn't think of anything heavier. After she had the sauce on, she went over and turned on the TV.

She didn't realize someone had boarded the boat and was now coming down the steps behind Paul, whose face she noticed was as colorless as white chalk. She stiffened and was alarmed as they walked over to where she sat. Her breath caught when she saw who was with Paul. There was no doubt in her mind that the man who stood looking down at her was none other than Jeff Owensford. At first glance, he looked so much like Brad they could be twins. She noticed his bluish-gray eyes that were so much like hers and Brads, but with one difference. Jeff's eyes were like cold steel. Emilia stared back at him defiantly. "So this is Emilia Wright," Jeff said. "You look just like your mother. She was very pretty too."

"How dare you keep me here against my will?" Emilia demanded. She waited for him to answer but he just continued to stare at her.

"You didn't answer me," she said angrily. "Why are you keeping me here?"

"I don't have to answer you," Jeff said. "You are in no position to demand anything." Emilia heard the coldness in his voice. It was evident he had no feeling for her even though she was his niece. She looked at Paul and was glad that he seemed to be in control of his emotions. Otherwise, they wouldn't have a chance.

"I think you are despicable," Emilia said. She got up to move away from him when he slapped her so hard across the face that she fell back down onto the chair. Emilia was shocked at how ruthless Jeff Owensford really was. She rubbed her check but was able to check the flow of tears she felt close to the surface. She wasn't going to give him the satisfaction of making her cry. She could see that Paul had clenched his fists. She gave him a warning look to keep his cool.

"You make sure you keep a civil tongue when you talk to me," Jeff said. "The next time I won't be so easy on you."

"How long are you staying?" Paul asked. Emilia listened intently for Jeff's answer.

"I believe I'll stay long enough to eat," Jeff said. "It smells pretty good and I did miss lunch. I'm sure Emilia would like me to stay. Isn't that right?" Emilia saw the naked hatred in his eyes when he looked at her. She decided her only course of action would be to agree with whatever he said. She did wonder if he was all there.

"Yes," Emilia said. "Perhaps you could tell me about the APLA." She sensed that Jeff wondered whether she was truly interested.

"Well, that's a little better," Jeff said. "I might talk to you about it while I eat. Then I'll have to leave for a while. I have a late appointment."

"Is there some special reason you came to the Cape?" Paul asked. Emilia could tell by watching Jeff's face that he didn't like being questioned.

"I wanted to check things out for myself," he said. "It seems to me you people are treating Emilia too well. She's not company, you know. She's your prisoner and must be treated like one." Emilia hoped and prayed he didn't intend to tie her up again. "Get that spaghetti on now," he said. "I don't have all day."

Emilia jumped up and went to turn on the burner under the water. She had no intention of provoking him. She realized Jeff Owensford was a very dangerous man and she knew that she and Paul would have to try and escape as soon as possible.

As Jeff ate, he talked a great deal about the APLA and their agenda. It was evident to Emilia that he sincerely pictured himself in control of the entire country someday in the very near future. She wondered if he suffered from some sort of delusional disorder, perhaps one of grandeur. She knew there were several types of delusional disorders, and although most presented symptoms at an early age, some can have an onset in later life. As Jeff grew more excited about his success, she noticed Paul also looked startled at Jeff's behavior.

"Does Brad know you belong to this organization?" Emilia asked. She wondered how he would react when he heard Brad's name.

Jeff laughed. "I'm sure he doesn't," he said. "He's so stupid, he probably wouldn't believe it even if he were told. I'd really like to see his face when he finds out. Better yet, when he finds out I'm responsible for your kidnapping. At last, I'll have my revenge."

"Revenge for what?" Emilia asked. "I don't understand."

"How could you?" Jeff snarled. "You weren't even thought of when Brad stole Katherine away from me. Oh, how I hated him for that. But I saw to it that he didn't marry her either. I went to a great deal of trouble to make sure. I got rid of anyone who knew Katherine was pregnant. I even killed the old lady to keep her quiet." Emilia didn't have to ask. She knew he was talking about her grandmother Emma. She remembered hearing somewhere that arsenic poisoning can mimic a heart attack. Emilia felt her insides shake and she felt sick to her stomach. She looked at Paul and sensed that he also realized what Jeff did but there was nothing he could do about it now.

After he finished eating, Jeff left and said he'd be back later tonight. Before Paul went up on deck, Emilia suggested to him that they wait until Jeff comes back before they attempt an escape. Paul then told Emilia about the strong medication Jeff took for his headaches. With luck, perhaps all three will be sleeping when they try to escape she thought. There was no question of making the attempt; it was just a question of when.

While Emilia finished cooking dinner, she indulged in fantasies of a successful escape where she reached the protection of a safe haven, preferably Brad's house. She looked forward to the blissful feeling of safety, which she always took for granted.

A large portion of spaghetti, followed by cake and ice cream for dessert, ought to make anyone sleepy she thought. She assumed Paul knew not to eat too much if he intended to have the stamina to row the boat. She was rather athletic, but hadn't worked out on a regular basis for some time. Although she wasn't sure exactly how far it was to Cape Cod Bay, she realized that from there it was still quite a distance down the beach to Brad's house.

Emilia wondered about Paul's physical fitness. After all, he was sixty-five years old and she had no idea if he engaged in some form of exercise on a regular basis or not. He appeared to be in very good shape for any age. We will have to rely on each other she thought.

When she called up that dinner was ready, the extra flow of adrenaline made her feel almost giddy. She realized she better hide such emotion or they might suspect she was up to something, especially Jake who even seemed a little leery of Paul.

When they came down the steps and sat down at the table, they appeared quite pleased with the dinner menu.

"This sure looks good," Carl said. "Spaghetti is one of my favorite foods."

"I'm glad," Emilia said. "A cook always enjoys hearing that her culinary efforts are appreciated." Emilia watched Carl pile it on his plate.

"I'm a little hungry myself," Jake said. "That ocean air really improves the appetite."

"Yes, it does," Paul agreed. "Unfortunately, I'm afraid I can't eat too much. My stomach's been bothering me lately." Emilia had wondered what excuse he would give.

"That's a bad break for you," Jake said. "This spaghetti is really good."

"Thanks," Emilia said. "There's a lot here, so help yourself."

The spaghetti turned out well, and Emilia would have eaten more had the circumstances been different. Paul also ate very little and turned down the dessert afterward. She made sure Jake and Carl got an extra large portion of cake and ice cream.

When they finished eating, Jake and Carl complained of being stuffed and feeling like they couldn't move. Emilia believed she had successfully motivated them toward napping. She anticipated that by the time it grew dark, they might doze off when she and Paul went up on deck. She hoped they would have enough time to row out of sight before Jake and Carl discovered they were gone.

After Emilia cleaned up the dishes, she turned on the evening news. They again reported that Emilia Wright was missing, showed her photograph and requested the public's assistance in locating her. In addition, there was now a $50,000 reward offered for any information leading to the apprehension of those who were responsible for her abduction. Emilia sensed that the news of the reward made Jake and Carl very uncomfortable. The weather report indicated a warm evening on tap, which was good news if you planned a late outing. Emilia saw Paul give her a nod, which was the signal that their escapade was about to commence.

"I'm going to take Emilia up on deck so she can get some air," Paul said. "We don't want her getting sick on us."

"Do you want Carl to go with you?" Jake asked. "I'm too full to move."

"No, that's not necessary," Paul replied. "She's not going to give me any trouble. She knows what will happen if she does. We'll be down in a little while."

"All right," Jake said. "Call if you want us."

Emilia told Carl there was an excellent old movie coming on in about fifteen minutes called "The Spiral Staircase" with Ethel Barrymore and George Brent. She said it was real scary and he shouldn't miss it. If Emilia was right, Jake would fall asleep and Carl would get so involved in the movie, he would forget all about her and Paul.

As they went up on deck, Emilia realized the chance they were taking, but it might turn out to be their only one.

They were only outside a few minutes when she saw someone walking along the dock toward the boat.

"Oh, no," Emilia said. "That looks like Jeff Owensford."

"It is," Paul said. "We'll just have to play if by ear."

"What are you two doing up here," Jeff demanded as he came on board. "Where are Jake and Carl?"

"We finished dinner a little while ago," Emilia said. "Jake is reading the paper and Carl is watching TV. They let me come up on deck last night after dark so I could get a little fresh air. It's so stuffy down there, they were afraid I'd get sick." She hoped Jeff would find that a legitimate reason for her being there.

"You can stay up here for a little while," Jeff said. "You make sure you watch her," he said to Paul. "I'm going inside to take my pill and lay down. Call me around 11:00."

Emilia waited for about thirty minutes. Then, she told Paul she was going down on the pretext of needing a sweater to see what they were doing. When she entered the cabin she noticed that Jeff had passed out on the bunk, Jake had fallen asleep reading the paper and Carl was so engrossed in the movie, he didn't even look up.

When Emilia went back up on deck, it was just beginning to get dark. She remembered the weatherman predicted a warm and clear night, which would afford them enough moonlight that they wouldn't find themselves engulfed in total darkness.

She saw that Paul had untied the dinghy and was waiting for her to help him lower it into the water. She nodded and whispered it was now or never.

"Is everything OK below?" Paul asked.

"Yes," Emilia whispered. "We won't have to change our plans at all. We'll lower the dinghy into the water, climb down the ladder and row our way close to the shoreline of the canal in the direction of Cape Cod Bay. Since we're docked close to the entrance of the canal, it won't take long to reach the Bay."

"Won't we be seen in the moonlight?" Paul asked.

"It's possible," Emilia said. "But there are many smaller boats on the canal. I don't think anyone will pay us much notice even if we are spotted. If we're lucky, we'll see the Coast Guard and hail them down."

"What if the others discover we're gone?" Paul asked. "They may even try to take the boat out to look for us." Emilia sensed that Paul was very apprehensive.

"I don't think they will look for us in the water," Emilia said. "At least not until they've searched for us around the marina. We can only hope they won't miss us for a while. Once we pass the power plant and leave the canal to enter Cape Cod Bay, it will probably be an hour before we can leave the water and go ashore onto the beach. I hope you're feeling energetic because this will probably take several hours." As they quietly spoke, Emilia and Paul lowered the dinghy into the water.

"Why couldn't we just try to get help from someone on another boat?" Paul asked. Emilia knew that there were a few boats docked in this area even though they were not in close proximity.

"Because they are just innocent bystanders, and we would be exposing them to potential danger, which is not something I want on my conscience," she replied. "I would rather we try to get away on our own."

"You're right," Paul said. "I hadn't given that much thought. This little excursion itself will not be dangerous, as long as we make it away from them."

"If this were the tourist season, we would have no problem finding help," Emilia said. "This is such a remote and unpopulated area the rest of the year."

"Don't worry," Paul said. "We'll make it."

"If we don't, I'll die fighting them before I let them tie me up again," Emilia said. "When you've never had a panic attack, you can't possibly understand what it's like."

"Oh, but I do understand," Paul said. "I've had a few myself. They say it's hereditary, so that must be additional confirmation that we are truly related."

"I don't doubt it at all," Emilia said. "My intuition was right on target as usual." Emilia carefully went down the ladder.

"Here, give me your hand," Paul said. "I'll help you into the boat."

Emilia felt immense relief as they rowed away from the shore and headed toward Cape Cod Bay. She looked up at the sky that was without a cloud and filled with millions of twinkling stars. Emilia wondered if perhaps Dennis was outdoors watching this same panorama while thinking of her. The sea was so calm, it was almost motionless, and all she could hear was the slapping noise of the oars as they made their way along the canal.

As Emilia continued to row, she filled Paul in on various events that happened to her over the years. She listened as Paul talked about his wife and their two children, who were two more cousins Emilia was unaware she had. She found it hard to believe that over the past week, she discovered a family she never knew existed: a father, two uncles, one aunt and three cousins.

Emilia heard the excitement in Paul's voice as he talked about the past he thought was lost to him forever. He told Emilia his philosophy was that everything that happens has a purpose and meaning, even though we may not see it at the time. Emilia asked him what purpose his amnesia had, and he told her he didn't know yet, but felt certain it would be revealed in time.

"How do you feel about Jeff Owensford now?" Emilia asked.

"You won't believe it," Paul replied. "I suddenly realized the bitterness is gone."

"How long do you think we've been out here?" Emilia asked. "It's really getting cold. I'm glad I used my sweater as a ruse to go down and check on those three or I wouldn't have it now."

"It's always cold on the ocean at night, especially at this time of year," Paul said. "It even gets chilly during the summer."

"I guess it's good in a way," Emilia said. "It will enable us to row longer, and harder, in an effort to stay warm. We should soon be coming to the Bay. I think those lights are guiding a large cargo ship that's probably just starting through the canal."

"Where do we go when we get to the Bay?" Paul asked.

"As soon as we pass the power plant on our right, we will be at the entrance to the Bay," Emilia replied. "Then we'll turn to the right and keep the boat close to the shoreline."

How long before we can go ashore onto the beach?" Paul asked.

"I think we should pass the posted preserve first," Emilia said. "Then we'll go ashore. I'll be glad to put my feet on dry land again, the sooner, the better."

"You did say Brad's house was located on the beach in East Sandwich, didn't you?" Paul asked.

"Yes, I did," Emilia replied. "If we continue down the beach past the preserve, we will end up at East Sandwich Beach."

"I can hardly believe it," Paul said.

Emilia could hardly believe it herself. The last two days, being held captive by Jake and Carl, felt more like two months.

"We're not out of the woods yet," Emilia said. "If they wake up and they can't find us around the marina, I'm sure they'll come looking out here."

"I don't even want to think about that," Paul said.

~ *TWENTY-THREE* ~

Even as Paul said the words, Jeff was waking up. He opened his eyes and looked around the cabin. It looked like Jake fell asleep reading the paper and Carl was sitting in front of the TV watching an old movie. Jeff got up and walked over to Carl.

"Where's Paul and Emilia," he asked. "Have they been down here at all?"

"I think Emilia came down for her sweater," Carl said. "That's the only time."

"I'm going up and check on them," Jeff said.

When Jeff went up on deck, he could see at once that Paul and Emilia were gone. He ran back down to the cabin to question Jake and Carl. Jeff saw that Jake was also awake now and figured Carl must have awakened him.

"They're not up there," Jeff shouted. "Did you hear anything at all?"

"No, I didn't," Jake said. "Where would they go?"

"I don't know, but Paul shouldn't have taken her off the boat," Jeff snarled. "Let's get the car and see if we can find them. She probably talked him into going for a walk."

"What will we do if we can't find them?" Jake asked.

"We've got to find them," Jeff said. "We'll have to keep looking until we do. Carl, you stay here in case they come back."

Jeff left the boat with Jake trailing behind. He walked to the end of the marina and then they got in the car. Jeff drove along the highway in both directions and saw no one out walking. He even went across the bridge, and still saw no one on foot.

Jeff noticed the small convenience store was still open. He went in, gave a brief description of Emilia and Paul, and inquired if his niece and brother had been in during the last thirty minutes. The clerk assured him he had but a handful of customers all evening, and no one fitting that description.

Jeff drove Jake back to the boat and told him and Carl to stay put until he returned. He drove around again looking for Paul and Emilia, but with no luck. Jeff wondered what was going on. Something just didn't seem right. He decided that this might be a good time to call Brad.

Jeff went to the phone booth at the end of the marina and dialed Brad's number.

When the phone rang, Dennis had just come in and Brad was watching the news. Dennis answered the phone and then told Brad it was for him. Dennis didn't recognize the voice, but he knew who it was by the look on Brad's face when he answered.

"Brad, this is Jeff," his brother said. "Were you expecting to hear from me?"

"What do you mean?" Brad asked.

"Well, I heard about Emilia being kidnapped," Jeff said. "After all, we are brothers. I thought you might need my help." Dennis poured himself some iced tea as he kept an eye on Brad. He could see that Brad looked absolutely astounded by whatever Jeff was saying.

"Just what kind of help can you give?" Brad asked.

"Wouldn't you like to get Emilia back?" Jeff asked.

"Jeff, where is she?" Brad demanded. "Why are you doing this to me? I don't understand." Dennis was standing by Brad's side trying to figure out what Jeff was saying to make Brad look as he did.

"I'm at home," Jeff said. "I'm controlling everything from right here. What is it you don't understand? You don't understand that I've hated you all my life, that I want to see you suffer, or that I want to see you destroyed. Which part is it you don't understand?" Dennis watched the color leave Brad's face as though from shock.

Then, Jeff began to laugh uncontrollably. Dennis listened as Brad held the phone out for him to hear. Dennis sensed that Brad now accepted the fact that there was something wrong with his brother. Dennis whispered to Brad to wait until Jeff stopped laughing before he tried to talk to him again.

"Jeff, what is it you want me to do?" Brad asked. "I'll do whatever you say."

"I'll call you tomorrow," Jeff said. "I'll give you a chance to think about it for a while."

"Please, Jeff, tell me where she is," Brad pleaded.

"I'll tell you tomorrow," Jeff said. "After you do what I want."

"I already told you I'd do whatever you say," Brad said.

Jeff laughed. "I know you will. But I want to enjoy this feeling for a while. Do you have any idea how long I've waited to get you where I have you now? This has been a wonderful night."

"Why?" Brad asked. "What makes tonight so wonderful?"

"I've finally brought you to your knees," Jeff said. "You said you would do anything I wanted, anything at all. Oh, I can't ever remember being as happy as I am tonight. You actually pleaded with me to tell you where Emilia is. Now I am the one in power, and you will do as I say."

"What will you do if the police find her?" Brad asked.

"Why would I tell you?" Jeff screamed. "You're nothing to me."

"What do you mean I'm nothing to you?" Brad asked. "I'm your brother. I can't believe I mean nothing to you."

"How can you believe you ever meant anything to me?" Jeff asked. "I don't give a hoot for you. I never have. I even made sure you never got Katherine or ever knew about Emilia. I couldn't believe you were so stupid that you never knew."

"You'll be the stupid one when they find Emilia," Brad said. "They already think they know where she is." Jeff could feel hot rage well up in him when Brad taunted him about the police finding Emilia.

"How could they know," Jeff snarled. "They don't even know I own a boat." As soon as the words came out of his mouth, Jeff realized he told Brad that Emilia was on his boat. He immediately hung up.

After Jeff Owensford hung up on Brad, he went back to the boat to see if Paul and Emilia ever showed up. There is something not quite right, he thought. He found Jake nervously pacing back and forth in the cabin while Carl was up on deck keeping watch. It was obvious that Paul and Emilia never came back.

"Did you notice anything funny going on between Paul and Emilia?" Jeff asked Jake. "Did they seem especially friendly?" He waited impatiently as Jake thought about it before answering.

"They were alone a few times," Jake said. "It seemed like they knew each other from before." Jeff wondered if Paul had regained his memory. That would explain why he and Emilia were gone. He also realized that he better get away from the boat and keep it under observation from somewhere else close by. He decided to go to the bar at the end of the marina where he could watch what went on without being seen. Before he left the boat, he told Jake that he and Carl should wait there until Paul and Emilia showed up.

~ TWENTY-FOUR ~

Dennis was alarmed about the way Brad looked when he hung up the phone. He quickly got Brad his glass and ordered him to take a drink. "What is it?" Dennis asked. "What did he say?"

"Joyce was right," Brad said. "There is definitely something wrong with Jeff."

"What did he say?" Dennis persisted.

"Besides revealing how much he hates me, he implied he's responsible for Emilia's abduction and will call tomorrow to let me know exactly what he wants in exchange for telling me where she is, although he did let it slip that she's on his boat."

"Where is he now?" Dennis asked.

"He said he was at home," Brad replied. "Maybe the police can do something?"

"No, we can't do that," Dennis said. "From what Joyce told you, he's liable to do anything, especially if he's pushed. I'm afraid we'll have to play the game as he calls it. At least, until we find out where he's taken Emilia."

"Shouldn't we let Chief Archer know what's happened?" Brad asked.

"We won't have to," Dennis said. "Remember, they have your phone tapped. But we'll call him and see what he thinks about the call."

When Dennis called the police station, they immediately put him through to Chief Archer.

"Chief, I guess you know about the call Brad just got from Jeff," Dennis said.

"Yes, I've just listened to it," Chief Archer said. "It sounds as though Jeff Owensford has about lost it."

"I wonder what he's got up his sleeve?" Dennis asked. "Why is he making Brad wait until tomorrow to hear what it is he wants? He also said he was calling from home. We know he's somewhere here on the Cape."

"Yes, he is," Chief Archer said. "But we don't know where. He wasn't on the phone long enough for us to trace the call. And that laugh is something else. It's enough to make your blood run cold."

"Yes, I know," Dennis said. "Anything new on where the boat might be docked?"

"Not yet," Chief Archer said. "I'll give you a call as soon as I know."

"I think I'll come over there now," Dennis said. "I want to be there when you find out."

"OK," Chief Archer said. "See you in a little while."

Dennis then told Brad he was going to the police station so he'd be there when they locate the boat. He said if Jeff calls again, Brad should promise to do whatever he wants. The best thing is to humor him but not in a patronizing way, which might only tend to infuriate him. Dennis then left to meet with Chief Archer.

When Dennis arrived at the police station, Chief Archer had just left a message for Agent Lawson to call. By the time Dennis got his coffee, Agent Lawson was on the line and the Chief put him on the speakerphone.

Dennis heard him say that the surveillance team reported that their search of Jeff's apartment had been unproductive and they thought it very probable that Emilia was indeed being held on Jeff's boat. He then asked if they knew yet where the boat was docked.

"Several people have been working on it," Chief Archer said. "Based on the progress made so far, they estimate it should take about another six hours to cover the entire list." Dennis paced around the office as he listened to their conversation.

"Is the list in alphabetical order or is it by area?" Dennis asked. "If it's by area, I would suggest they concentrate on those located closest to Sandwich and work out from there. Since the Owensfords are originally from the Sandwich area, it's quite likely they've used the same docking facility for years."

"Offhand, I'm not sure how the list was requested from the computer programmer," Chief Archer said. "I'll check on it, and if it's not by area, I'll have them run one that is, making sure to eliminate those facilities that have already been contacted. Then we can start again by area."

Dennis was glad to hear that Agent Lawson wanted to be notified as soon as they located the boat and that they have a team on standby waiting for the call. Dennis agreed with Agent Lawson that if they had been able to obtain an order to tap Jeff Owensford's phone, they would probably know where he was now.

"I'll get back to you when I have the information," Chief Archer said as he hung up the phone.

Dennis called Agent Lawson about thirty minutes later. "We've located the boat," he said. "It's docked at a marina in the canal, not too far from the entrance at Cape Cod Bay. How do you want to proceed?"

"I'll notify the team we have on standby," Agent Lawson said. "They have already been instructed not to make contact, but to secure the area, block all exits and wait until we get there."

"Do you want us to pick you up on the way?" Dennis asked.

"Yes, that will save time," Agent Lawson said. "You and Chief Archer are more familiar with the area."

Dennis called Brad on his car phone as he and Chief Archer sped toward the rendezvous point where they were to pick up Agent Lawson. "Brad, I don't have any time to talk," Dennis said. "I wanted you to know we've located the boat and we're on our way. Don't leave the house. I'll get back to you as soon as possible."

"Thanks," Brad said. "Please call as soon as you can."

When Dennis arrived at the scene, Agent Lawson's men were already in the process of completely surrounding the entire area and blocking both ends of the road leading onto the dock. The entire operation took approximately five minutes and everyone was in place.

Dennis noticed Howard McMillen and went over to him. "I didn't know you still worked for the FBI," he said.

"Officially, I'm retired," Howard said. "Agent Lawson knows how close Bill Stewart and I are, so when I asked to be assigned to the case, he pulled some strings and got an OK. I want to help get the one who almost killed Bill, and make sure he's put away for a long time."

"Have you seen anyone on the boat?" Dennis asked.

"No," Howard replied. "It's been quiet since we got here. They must still be up because the light in the cabin is on and we do see movement. By the rhythmic interruption of the light coming from the cabin, it looks as though someone is pacing back and forth."

Dennis heard Agent Lawson ask someone for a bullhorn. "We may as well let them know we are here, and see if they'll surrender peacefully," he said.

"Wouldn't it be better to try to sneak onto the boat?" Dennis asked.

"The feasibility of successfully sneaking onto a boat that size is practically nil," Agent Lawson said. "I'd rather try it this way, and maybe nobody will get hurt."

"It's your play," Dennis said. "My only concern is that Emilia doesn't get hurt."

"I understand that," Agent Lawson said. "They know it will be worse for them if she does, which normally proves to be a deterrent."

Dennis watched Agent Lawson turn the bullhorn on.

"You, in there!" Agent Lawson enunciated. "You're surrounded. Come out with your hands up."

Dennis listened as Agent Lawson used the bullhorn again.

"You must come out with your hands up," Agent Lawson said. "You must comply. You are surrounded. You cannot escape."

"What happens next?" Dennis asked.

"We give them a little time to think about it," Agent Lawson said. "Then we tell them to surrender again. We don't want to storm the boat and risk any loss of life. We'll continue to use the bullhorn for a while and let them stew."

"Do you think they'll come out?" Dennis asked.

"They usually do," Agent Lawson said. "Of course, it isn't possible to predict how uniquely different individuals will react when facing similar circumstances. We can only hope."

As Dennis watched, the light in the cabin went out. He heard the bullhorn sound again.

"Send Emilia out unharmed and it will go easier for you," Agent Lawson said. "Send her out now."

Dennis thought he saw someone move on the deck. "What was that noise?" he asked. "It sounded like someone knocking."

"I didn't hear anything," Agent Lawson said. "Did you hear anything, Chief?"

"I heard something," Chief Archer said. "I don't know what it was, and I can't see anything."

All of a sudden, the roar of the engine filled the quiet night and Dennis watched as the boat pulled away from the dock and quickly picked up speed. He heard Agent Lawson immediately get on the radio to notify the Coast Guard. Dennis watched as the boat sped through the dark murky waters, and he could hear the eerie siren of the Coast Guard boat as he saw them in relentless pursuit.

Chief Archer and Dennis stood together at the edge of the dock watching as the Coast Guard began to gain on them. Then Dennis caught sight of the media as they arrived on the scene.

"Oh, no," Dennis said. "Looks like somebody tipped them off."

"They're like vultures," Agent Lawson said. "They can smell blood, and they're right there, shoving their cameras in the face of victims. Howard, keep those reporters back," he shouted. "Don't give them any information. Tell them I'll give them a statement later."

"It looks like the Coast Guard has almost caught up to them," Dennis said. "They're almost to the entrance of the canal."

Suddenly, Dennis realized that the boat accelerated and gained speed just as a large cargo ship was being guided into the canal. The small boat seemed to be out of control and was headed directly into the cargo ship's path.

Dennis watched in horror as the boat being chased by the Coast Guard crashed into the cargo ship, exploded and burst into flames. He couldn't imagine how anyone on the smaller boat could have survived. He felt a numbness go through him.

"I never expected that," Agent Lawson said. "Never in a million years."

"The speed probably caused him to lose control," Chief Archer said. "It takes a bit of skill to maneuver a boat that size, and he may not have been able to handle it."

Dennis saw Howard look his way. "Do you think it's possible anyone survived?" he asked.

"It doesn't look good," Agent Lawson said. "Not at all."

"How long will they continue to search?" Dennis asked." He could hear his voice break with emotion.

"From what we saw, I don't believe they'll search much longer tonight," Agent Lawson said. "I imagine they'll begin again tomorrow morning, but this time they'll be searching for bodies I'm sorry to say."

"I better get over to Brad's house before he hears it on the radio," Dennis said. "I don't know what I'm going to say." Dennis was still numb with shock as he slowly walked down the dock to his car. He heard Agent Lawson run to catch up with him.

"We can't be positive of anything yet," he said. "We aren't even absolutely certain Emilia was on the boat. All the information we have in that regard is a demented individual's statement that she was. We didn't actually see her. There is still hope."

~ TWENTY-FIVE ~

As Dennis arrived at Brad's house, he noticed the lights were on and knew that Brad must still be up. Brad heard the car pull up and was at the door before Dennis had a chance to ring the bell.

"What's happened?" Brad asked. "I heard something on the radio about an accident in the canal. Dennis could see that Brad was extremely excited.

"Let's go in and sit down and I'll fill you in," Dennis said. They went into the living room and Dennis paused at the window for a few minutes and looked out at the ocean as he struggled to keep his own emotions under control. Then when they sat down on the sofa, Dennis reluctantly began to tell Brad what happened.

"We had the dock sealed off," he said. "Agent Lawson used a bullhorn about three times to order them out. Then we heard some kind of knocking noise and they suddenly pulled away from the dock, quickly accelerated and gained speed. The Coast Guard was in pursuit when Jeff's boat ran into a huge cargo ship. His boat exploded on impact, and burst into flames."

"Oh, no!" Brad exclaimed. "How could you have let that happen?"

"I'm sorry," Dennis said. "I wasn't in charge, but I don't think it would have made any difference. There was nothing else we could have done. We never took any aggressive action against them. We only told them to come out with their hands up. We made no attempt to rush the boat, nor was Agent Lawson contemplating any such action. I think they simply panicked and decided to make a run for it."

"Do you think there's any possibility there were survivors?" Brad whispered.

"It doesn't look good," Dennis said. "They were still searching the water when I left. I wanted to talk to you myself before you heard it on the radio."

"They shouldn't have gone after them," Brad shouted. "They should have let me deal with Jeff myself to get her back." Dennis watched in anguish as Brad paced back and forth and continued to shout.

"Now she's dead," Brad cried out. "I'll kill him." Dennis could see that Brad was overwrought and about to break down.

"Brad, we're not even sure Emilia was on the boat," Dennis said. "Remember how crazy Jeff was talking? He could have been lying to you. We never saw her."

Dennis paused and waited as Brad weighed his words. "You're right," he said. "I don't believe she was on the boat. I won't believe it. I'm sorry. I tell everyone to remain in control and be optimistic, and then I completely go off the deep end. I'm sure Agent Lawson did what he thought best. I won't give up hope either."

Even though Brad calmed down, Dennis felt certain that he would kill Jeff without hesitation if anything happened to Emilia.

"I'm going back now," Dennis said. "I'll definitely keep in touch. Why don't you try to get some sleep."

"I won't be able to," Brad said. "I'll be waiting to hear from you."

When Dennis got back to the dock, he saw that Agent Lawson was giving a statement to the reporters on the scene. Dennis listened as he told them the FBI was there in response to an anonymous tip that Emilia Wright was being held on the boat involved in the accident. There was nothing further he could tell them, he said, until they had exhausted every effort in their search for survivors. They clamored for more, but Agent Lawson walked away. Dennis knew he was not particularly enamored with the media in general.

"How did Brad take the news?" Agent Lawson asked.

"Not too well at first, but then he settled down," Dennis said. "I felt sorry for him. You don't know how much I'm counting on what I told him, that Jeff was lying about Emilia being on the boat. I could strangle him myself."

"Is that what Brad threatened to do?" Agent Lawson asked. "I wouldn't blame him either."

"Is it possible Jeff was also on the boat?" Dennis asked.

"Right now, we don't know who was on the boat," Agent Lawson said. "There are five people we can't account for. There's Emilia, Paul, Jeff and the two kidnappers. So far, we haven't recovered a single person, dead or alive."

"I wonder if Chief Archer put out an APB on Jeff Owensford?" Dennis asked. "Maybe I should call the station and see."

"Maybe you should wait until morning," Agent Lawson said. "It's almost one-thirty."

"I didn't realize it was that late," Dennis said. "I guess we could all use a little sleep. You want me to drop you off?"

"No, thanks," Agent Lawson said. "I'll ride back to the motel with Howard McMillen. I'll see you in the morning."

"Good," Dennis said. "Call me if there's any news before then. I'm going back to Brad's house."

"I will," Agent Lawson said. "Thanks for all your help."

"No problem," Dennis said. "Anytime." Dennis wondered if Brad would still be up when he got back to the house.

- *TWENTY-SIX* -

Emilia and Paul had passed the entrance to Cape Cod Bay when they heard the explosion. Emilia jumped as the noise of the blast shattered the stillness. "What was that!" she cried out. When she stopped rowing and looked back, she saw a red glow that lit up the sky over the huge cargo ship they just passed a few minutes earlier as it entered the canal.

"It looks like there was some kind of accident on the cargo ship," Paul said. "That red glow and black smoke is almost certainly emanating from a fire. I wonder what happened? Perhaps they hit something in the water."

"Maybe something on board exploded," Emilia said. "They may be carrying chemicals or something very explosive in nature. Whatever it was, the ship must not have suffered any mechanical damage. It looks as though it's continuing on."

"Yes, it does seem to be moving again," Paul agreed.

"I guess we better do the same," Emilia said. "I'll be glad to get my feet back on dry land."

"Where is the preserve you told me about?" Paul asked.

"We should be coming to it soon," Emilia said. "Then we'll go ashore and walk down the beach. We better stay close to the grassy hillside so we can't be spotted."

"Do you think that's really necessary?" Paul asked. "Would they come out here on the beach at night to look for us?"

"I wouldn't put anything past them," she replied. "It's better to be on the safe side. Jeff Owensford has a lot at stake here."

It was approximately two-fifteen in the morning when Emilia and Paul went ashore, and they were exhausted. They walked across the beach to the grassy hillside and sat down. Emilia briskly rubbed her arms.

"My arms are aching already," she said. "I can imagine what they'll feel like tomorrow."

"This is definitely not something I'd like to do every day," Paul said. "Perhaps we better sit and rest for a while before we continue down the beach."

"Sounds good to me," Emilia said. "It's so quiet, except for the sounds of the sea. If it weren't so cold, I'd probably fall asleep. You must be freezing in that short sleeved shirt."

"I am a little cold," Paul admitted. "But I'm used to it, as Janet will tell you. She calls me a fresh air freak. Even in the dead of winter, I prefer having a window open in my bedroom."

"I'm like that myself," Emilia said. "As long as there's a blanket to crawl under to keep warm."

"How do you like the Cape?" Paul asked.

"I like it a lot," Emilia replied. "My mother grew up here, and I've always lived in Plymouth, which is only about thirty minutes away. Actually, you were born here, too. Do you remember growing up here?"

"I think I'm beginning to," Paul said. "I'm sure it will eventually all come back. That's the way the doctor told me it would probably happen, in bits and pieces. It's amazing the way the human brain stores unlimited knowledge in the subconscious, and then suddenly releases the desired information with no apparent motivation other than powerful emotion. At least, that appears to be the trigger which has activated mine."

"It certainly reaffirms the fact that one should never give up hope," Emilia said.

"Yes, it does," Paul said. "I must admit, I was almost to the point of giving up hope that my memory would ever be restored."

"Well, do you feel rested enough to go on?" Emilia asked.

"Yes, I'm fine," Paul said. "We only have a short way to go from here, don't we?"

"Yes, it will probably take an hour or so," Emilia said. "In fact, from Brad's house, on a clear night, you can make out the lights on the large stack of the power plant."

Do you suppose Jeff is awake yet?" Paul asked. "Maybe he's already sent Jake and Carl to look for us."

"I have a feeling they know by now we're gone," Emilia said. "I would guess they are out looking for us. That's why we better not walk along the shoreline, but rather next to the grassy area. We'll be much harder to spot that way. The walking might be a little easier, too. There are an awful lot of stones by the water's edge."

"But the sand's deeper here," Paul said. "So I don't expect it to be a time-saving advantage."

Emilia and Paul walked slowly and warily down the beach toward the point where they believed Brad's house to be. The beach at night was very dark and lonely, much different than it was during the day. Emilia was glad it was a clear night. She could imagine what it would be like if it were cloudy and dark, with no stars twinkling above. You probably wouldn't be able to see your hand in front of your face she thought.

Dennis and Brad were also outdoors looking up at the stars. When Dennis got back to the house, he found Brad sitting out on the back deck deep in his own thoughts. In fact, Dennis startled him when he opened the sliding glass doors to join him. Then they both just sat quietly listening to the soothing sounds of the ocean.

"Are you going to bed?" Dennis asked. "Or are you going to sit here all night?"

"I think I'm going to sit here until I get an answer," Brad replied. "If I go to bed, I'll just toss and turn. I won't be able to sleep."

"I don't think I could either," Dennis said. "When I sit out here on a clear night like this, and look up at the sky, I realize I'm just a minute dot in the whole scheme of things. It invariably emphasizes how insignificant I am, and helps me to accept and put things in the proper perspective."

"Oh, now you're getting philosophical like me," Brad said. "It takes a lot to develop a capacity for reasoning during difficult times."

"Sometimes I think we must reach the point of acceptance before God intervenes," Dennis said. "I think I've reached that point, and I pray that He will intervene and make things right."

"Amen," Brad softly whispered.

"I'm going for a walk on the beach," Dennis said. "I'd ask you to join me, but one of us should be here in case the phone rings."

"All right," Brad said. "You go ahead. If I hear anything, I'll come after you."

Dennis went down the steps to the beach, and began to briskly walk along the shoreline. If I walk to the preserve and back, I'll get tired enough to sleep, he thought.

After Dennis walked about thirty minutes, he thought he saw something moving toward him, but away from the shoreline. He immediately stopped, and strained his eyes trying to focus on what he'd seen. Strain as he would, he saw nothing moving. He continued to slowly walk, but didn't take his eyes off the area where he noticed the movement. Sure enough, he saw it again. He didn't know whether to turn back or continue on, since he was absolutely sure someone or some thing was just up ahead.

Meanwhile, Emilia also noticed a figure walking toward them, but along the shoreline. "What should we do?" she whispered.

"I'm not sure," Paul said. "From the silhouette, I don't think it's Jake or Carl."

"Perhaps we should just continue walking," Emilia said.

As Dennis walked nearer and his eyes were able to focus on the area, he realized the movement was two people walking down the beach. He thought it odd, since most walkers preferred to walk along the shoreline. He decided to call out and acknowledge their presence. I will know then whether they're out for a walk, or perhaps lost, he thought.

"Hello," Dennis called out. "Is someone there?"

"Dennis, is that you?" Emilia cried. She left Paul and began running down the beach toward Dennis. He could hardly believe his eyes when he saw Emilia running toward him.

"Thank God, Emilia, we didn't know if you were dead or alive," Dennis said as he held out his arms and caught her, lifting her off the ground. "Oh, Emilia, I was so afraid I'd lost you," he whispered in her ear as he held her in his arms and kissed her over and over. "Please don't ever leave me again. I don't know what I'd do without you."

"Denny, I was so afraid," Emilia said. "Afraid I was never going to see you again. Thoughts of you and our future together are what got me through it. I love you so much."

"I love you, too," Dennis whispered, completely oblivious to Paul who walked up behind them. Then Emilia and Dennis heard Paul discreetly cough.

"I'm sorry to intrude," Paul said. Dennis turned to look at Paul who somehow looked familiar although Dennis was sure they'd never met.

"Dennis, do you remember when I told you about my Uncle Andrew?" Emilia asked. "This is he, alias Paul Freedman."

"Yes, I do," Dennis said as he shook Paul's hand. "Although I never thought I'd see you again. How in the world did the two of you get out here?"

"It's a long story," Emilia said. The three of them headed back down the beach, this time walking along the shoreline. "Where is Brad?" she asked.

"He's sitting out on the back deck," Dennis said. "I left him there while I went for a walk. Neither one of us could sleep. We were worried sick about you. Jeff, who we think has some delusional disorder, told us he was responsible for having you abducted, and that you were being held captive on his boat. When Chief Archer discovered the location of the boat, we went there. Agent Lawson ordered everyone to come out with their hands up. We didn't even know for sure who was on the boat, when it suddenly pulled away from the dock and took off at great speed. With the Coast Guard in pursuit, the boat went out of control, and slammed into a large cargo ship. The boat exploded on impact. The Coast Guard and a helicopter searched for survivors, but none were found.

"So that's why you thought I was dead," Emilia said.

"Yes, we thought you were on the boat," Dennis said.

"Paul and I were both on the boat," she said. "But last night, we escaped by lowering the dinghy and rowing through the canal and out into the Bay. In fact, we passed the cargo ship that was involved in the accident. We just entered Cape Cod Bay when we heard the explosion and saw the red glow and the smoke. We assumed something on the cargo ship exploded. We never for one minute connected it to the boat we were on. We came ashore, rested for a while, and then started to walk down the beach."

"Who was on the boat?" Dennis asked.

"When we left the boat, Jeff Owensford and Jake Powell were asleep and Carl Matthews was watching TV," Emilia said.

As the three of them neared the house, Emilia looked up and saw Brad standing at the railing. It looked like he was straining to see who was doing all the talking. When she ran up the steps calling his name, Emilia noticed he looked at her in disbelief and seemed unable to move. She ran over and hugged him.

"Oh, Emilia," Brad said with a break in his voice. "I'm so glad you're safe." She put her arm around him as they walked into the house. The four of them went into the living room and sat down.

"The first thing I want to do is take a shower," Emilia said. "Then I think I'll probably sleep for two or three days."

"I think I'll call Chief Archer," Dennis said.

"Don't you think you should wait until morning?" Emilia asked. "He's probably sleeping."

"I don't think he'll mind when he hears why I'm calling," Dennis said.

Dennis heard the annoyance in Chief Archer's voice when he answered the phone.

"Chief Archer, it's Dennis McClelland," he said. "Emilia is here. She and Paul Freedman are both here."

"What did you say?" Chief Archer asked. "Did I hear you right, or am I still dreaming?"

"No, you're not dreaming," Dennis said. "You heard me right. Emilia and Paul Freedman are both here."

"That's wonderful news," Chief Archer said. "How in the world did they get away? Or weren't they on the boat?"

"They were on the boat," Dennis said. "But they escaped before we got there." Dennis then told Chief Archer how they managed to get away and make it to Brad's house.

"How fortunate and timely their escape turned out to be," Chief Archer said. "If they had remained on the boat, they might have been killed."

"That was too close for comfort," Dennis said. "I guess I should notify Agent Lawson too. I want to let him know that Emilia said Jeff Owensford was on the boat with the two kidnappers when she and Paul got away. I'll talk to you later. Sorry I woke you up."

After Dennis hung up, he picked up the drink Brad sat down on the table next to the phone while he talked to Chief Archer. He saw that Emilia, Brad and Paul were sitting on the other side of the room catching up as he dialed Agent Lawson's number.

Although half asleep when he answered, Dennis sensed that Agent Lawson was wide-awake after hearing his news about Emilia and Paul.

"You never know, do you?" Agent Lawson said. "Didn't I tell you we couldn't be certain she was on the boat?"

"Yes, you did," Dennis said. "But you didn't really believe it, did you?"

"No, I've got to admit I didn't," Agent Lawson replied. "I suppose I'll have to let the media know that Emilia has been found."

"I also wanted to let you know that Emilia said Jeff Owensford was on the boat with the two kidnappers when she and Paul got away," Dennis said. "So it looks like our troubles are over."

"It appears so," Agent Lawson agreed. "We'll see if we can recover the bodies in the morning. Well, thanks for calling, and good luck."

"Thank you," Dennis said as he hung up the phone and went to join the others.

"What about Joyce?" Dennis asked. "Do you think we should call and let her know before she hears it on the news?"

"Let's wait until morning," Emilia said. "We really won't know for sure about the three on the boat until their bodies are found."

"I think Emilia is right," Brad said. "It can wait until morning. I can hardly believe Jeff is gone." Emilia heard the sadness in Brad's voice despite all that Jeff did to him over the years. Emilia found it hard to feel sorrow over Jeff Owensford's death, but then she had only seen his worst side. She did feel sympathy for Brad and she put her arm around him in support.

TWENTY-SEVEN

Jeff Owensford could see from his vantage point that everyone left the dock except for one policeman who was left to stand guard over the scene. Lucky for him his suspicion that something was not right turned out to be true or he would be floating in the sea now along with Jake and Carl. He also realized that by now they probably believe him to be dead also. They will soon discover they are wrong he thought as he walked toward the main road to look for a cab. It soon dawned on him how deserted the area was and he would be hard pressed to find a cab out here.

Jeff's rental car was still parked on the street above the road leading to the dock. He wondered if it were possible during all the confusion that the car was never noticed. It was not unusual for people to park rental cars near the dock when they left in their boats. He decided to take the chance. He walked to the car, got in and drove up to the main highway. He didn't see or hear anything move, so he knew his instinct was right.

As Jeff drove to 6A and headed toward the turn off to Brad's house, he wondered if Brad and those staying with him were now asleep. He was pretty sure Emilia and Paul would be there. He remembered the housekeeper used to arrive early. He would be able to get in when she turned off the alarm to open the door.

When Jeff arrived at Brad's house, it was about 6:00 a.m. He pulled his car around to the far side of the house behind some large pine trees and out of sight. Then he waited in the wooded area directly across the road from the front entrance for the housekeeper to arrive. If Brad's routine was the same as the last time he was here, he expected her to arrive about 6:30 and go directly to the kitchen to start breakfast.

Jeff was not disappointed. He watched as she turned off the alarm and entered the house. He waited about five minutes, then walked to the front door and cautiously opened it and quietly stepped inside.

He read a note on the table in the hall, which informed the housekeeper that they would probably be sleeping late. Brad gave instructions to have the coffee ready, but he would let her know what time he wanted breakfast served. Jeff took note that there would be four for breakfast.

Jeff felt sure that Emilia and Paul were here, but he wondered who the other person might be. Then he remembered hearing that Emilia and Dennis McClelland were an item, so he figured it might well be Dennis McClelland. He sensed they were all still asleep. There was no sound at all except for the housekeeper in the kitchen.

Jeff wondered where he could hide while he waited to deal with them one at a time. He decided to go upstairs to the small linen room at the top of the steps. That way, after they were all downstairs, he could stand in the shadows of the hallway where he could hear where they were and what was being said.

Jeff no sooner crept up the steps and into the linen room with the louvered door he could see through, than he saw Brad leave his room, come down the hall and start down the steps. He noticed how well and happy Brad looked. Of course, he would; he thinks I'm dead Jeff thought. His hatred was so intense his stomach twisted into a hard knot that almost doubled him over.

About ten minutes later, Jeff saw Paul as he started down the steps. He planned to finish the job he started on him some forty years ago. Only this time, Paul would know who was trying to kill him. Jeff couldn't stand the sight of him. He never could. It was probably all Paul's doing that his plans fell apart. Jeff suddenly realized he'd better remain calm or his headache might return. Luckily, his pills were in his pocket if he needed them.

Jeff waited another thirty minutes before Emilia went down. It was true. She was very pretty. She looked like Katherine. Jeff smiled at the thought of Katherine. But the smile soon changed to a frown. Katherine had rejected him for Brad. She alone had caused this whole thing Jeff reasoned. Now Emilia would have to pay. There had to be retribution Jeff thought. He must be avenged for what they'd done to him.

His thoughts were interrupted as he watched Dennis walk toward the steps. This must be Dennis McClelland, the private investigator, who works for Brad he thought. Now, he is in love with Emilia as I once was with Katherine. It's sad they, too, will never find happiness he thought. He didn't want to hurt them, but he had no choice.

Jeff stepped out of the room and listened at the top of the steps. He could hear them in the dining room waiting for breakfast.

"Brad, did you call Joyce?" Emilia asked.

"Yes, I did," he said. "She said she could come over. She'll probably be here in about ten minutes."

They just started to eat breakfast when the doorbell rang and Brad's housekeeper showed Joyce into the dining room. Emilia noticed Joyce looked a little strained as though she hadn't slept well.

"Sit down and join us for breakfast," Emilia said. She introduced Paul to Joyce as she sat down next to him.

"Thank you," Joyce said. "I've already eaten, but I'll have a cup of coffee. I'm so glad you're all right, Emilia. I heard the news on the radio this morning, although they didn't give any details."

That's why we asked you to come over," Brad said. "Emilia will tell you what happened."

Emilia told Joyce how she and Paul had escaped and found their way back to Brad's house. She didn't mention Jeff's part in all of it. Emilia thought it would be better if Brad told her about her father.

"That was some experience," Joyce said.

"I'm afraid there's more," Brad said. "It's not going to be easy to tell you." Emilia sensed Brad's reluctance to hurt Joyce.

"What is it?" Joyce asked.

"It's about your father," Brad said. "I'm afraid he was the one responsible for Emilia's abduction, even though he was not actively involved. I wanted you to know that before you hear it on a news broadcast." Emilia could see the denial on Joyce's face as she began to protest.

"But why would my father do such a thing?" Joyce asked. "Emilia is his own niece."

"We think he developed some sort of delusional disorder," Brad said. "You know he was not himself for quite some time." Emilia gave Dennis a nod to help Brad.

"I'm afraid your father is also the one who's blackmailed Brad all these years," Dennis said. "His investment brokerage business is only a front he uses to conceal his affiliation with the APLA." Emilia saw tears fill Joyce's eyes and silently stream down her face.

"I'm finding this difficult," Joyce said with a broken voice. "What you're asking me to believe is that my father is a psychopathic liar, who has successfully lived a double life for years. In the process, he's manipulated several others to be active participants in various criminal offenses, the latest being the abduction of Emilia. Is that correct?" Emilia heard the defiance in her voice.

"Joyce, I know this is hard for you to accept," Brad said. "I didn't want to believe it either, but it is true. Your father told me, himself, that he was responsible for Emilia's abduction. The assailants held her prisoner on your father's boat. Paul has worked for your father for years, and he just found out a few days ago that Jeff tried to have him killed. Remember how difficult he's been to talk to lately? That's because this disorder he has is worsening. Didn't Dr. Scott tell you if he didn't get medication, he might harm himself as well as others?"

"Yes, he did," Joyce said. "I still find it hard to believe."

"There is more," Emilia said. "This will be the hardest part to hear. Your father was on the boat when Paul and I escaped. We don't know for sure, but it is possible he was killed when his boat hit the other ship last night."

Emilia sensed her pain as Joyce broke down and cried. She got up and went around to the other side of the table and put her arms around her. "Come on, Joyce," Emilia said. "Let's go in the living room and sit down. Dennis, would you bring our coffee in there?"

Jeff heard the whole thing from his position at the top of the steps. He peeked over the rail as Emilia and Joyce walked through the front hall to the living room. When Joyce broke down and sobbed, it did something to him. He leaned back against the wall for support. For the first time in his life, he felt sorry that he'd hurt someone. He was numb with the realization that Joyce really cared for him. He wondered why he ever felt otherwise. Perhaps they were right. Maybe he was becoming unhinged. Or maybe this is all just a trick he thought. They might all be pretending to be sorry that he's dead. Of course, that must be it.

After a few minutes, Joyce left and Emilia went back to the dining room to join the others. This time when the doorbell rang, it was Chief Archer and Agent Lawson.

"Come in," Brad said. "Would you like a cup of coffee?"

"No, thank you," Chief Archer said. "We just came to let you know we found the bodies of Jake Powell and Carl Matthews this morning. There was no sign of Jeff Owensford yet."

"Then, it's possible he wasn't on the boat," Emilia said. "Maybe he left after Paul and I escaped." She felt a sudden chill go through her at the possibility that Jeff Owensford was still alive and capable of hurting them.

"I doubt it," Agent Lawson said. "But there is that possibility. That's why I'm assigning a couple of men for surveillance until we know one way or the other."

"Thank you," Emilia said. "That will make us feel better."

Brad walked them to the door. When he returned, Emilia and Dennis asked Brad and Paul if they'd like to join them for a walk on the beach. Paul said he was going to call a cab to take him to the airport. He wanted to get home and let Janet, his wife, know that he was all right.

"I'll just stick with Paul until his cab comes," Brad said. "Then I might come out on the deck for a while."

"We'll say goodbye then," Emilia said. "I hope you'll come and see us soon." She gave Paul a hug.

"I will," Paul said. "I want you to meet the rest of my family. I'll give you a call next week."

"We'll see you later," Emilia said as she and Dennis went out the sliding glass doors onto the deck.

Jeff watched from the top of the steps as Brad and Paul went into the living room. He heard Paul call for a cab. Jeff realized he would probably have to let Paul leave. He wasn't up to taking on Brad and Paul at the same time. He could always make a phone call to take care of Paul. But he definitely wanted to take care of Brad in person.

It was about fifteen minutes later when the cab driver rang the bell. Brad walked Paul to the door and they shook hands before Paul got into the cab. Jeff then heard the sliding glass doors and knew that Brad must have gone out on the deck. He wondered where the housekeeper was.

He quietly made his way down the steps and noticed the basement door was open. He listened and could hear the washer and dryer running and realized the housekeeper was probably down there doing the laundry. He quietly went down the steps and saw her loading more clothes into the washer.

Her back was to him. He picked up a large flashlight from the shelf next to him and ran toward her. She turned at the sound and raised her arms to fend him off, but it was too late. She never had a chance. Jeff struck her with all his might on the side of her head and she fell to the basement floor. He could see the blood gush out from the wound and it splattered the side of the washer and dryer. He knew she would not be warning anyone of his presence.

He went back upstairs and locked the basement door behind him. Now, he would somehow have to lure Brad back into the house. Perhaps a noise might do the trick he thought. He could drop something or knock over a chair. Brad might think his housekeeper needed help. Jeff went into the kitchen and picked up a vase from the table and threw it to the floor. The sound of glass breaking was unmistakable. He heard Brad call out to ask what the noise was all about. Jeff knew Brad would be coming in any minute to investigate. He hid behind the kitchen door and waited.

Brad came through the door and looked around the kitchen. Then Jeff closed the door and stood in front of it, blocking Brad's way. He watched as the color quickly drained from Brad's face. Jeff could almost smell the fear.

"My God," Brad said. "What have you done? How did you get that blood on you?" Jeff looked down and saw that he did indeed have blood on the front of his shirt and pants. "Where's my housekeeper?"

Jeff laughed in a cackling way. "Oh, she won't be bothering us," he said. "She may never bother anyone again."

"What do you want?" Brad asked. "What are you going to do?"

"I think we'll just wait until Emilia comes back," Jeff said. "Then I'll have my revenge." Jeff watched Brad's face turn even whiter as he threatened to harm Emilia."

"Revenge for what?" Brad shouted. "I don't understand why you hate me so?"

Jeff quickly stepped to the side as Brad moved toward him. He drew a gun from his jacket and pointed it at Brad. "Now, you go over there and sit down," Jeff snarled. "Or I'll shoot you where you stand." As soon as Brad sat down on the chair, Jeff hit him on the back of his head and he slumped forward at the table. Jeff then grabbed a kitchen towel from the counter and he leaned Brad back in the chair and tied his hands behind his back.

"Now, all we have to do is wait for Emilia and Dennis to come back," Jeff said out loud to himself. "Then the party can begin."

- *TWENTY-EIGHT* -

Emilia and Dennis walked along the shoreline almost as far as the preserve. A large sandbar had come up and they took off their shoes and went out to look for shells. Emilia sensed how relaxed Dennis was as they leisurely strolled hand in hand along the edge of the sandbar. Right now, she felt as though she didn't have a care in the world. It had been one bizarre week she thought. Then she listened as Dennis voiced the same sentiment as though reading her mind.

"This has been one hell of a week," Dennis said. "It's hard to believe so much could happen in one week, both good and bad."

"I know," she agreed. "I feel as though I've matured in so many ways. I was rather intolerant about a lot of things before last week. In fact, I was downright smug and pig headed."

"Don't be so hard on yourself," Dennis said. "We all have our own little idiosyncrasies."

"Yes, and the older we get, the more engrained they become," Emilia said. "I certainly was wrong about Brad. I hope I always remember to have all my facts straight before I presume to make a judgement about something. I think I learned a lot from this experience, but it was sure a hard lesson."

"I would say you were on a fast roller coaster last week," Dennis said. "But you hung on and finished the ride and I'm proud of you." He put his arm around her as they continued their walk.

"I guess maybe we should start back," she said. "I don't want to leave Brad alone too long. He's had a bad time of it. I can't pretend I cared much for Jeff Owensford but he was Brad's brother. Actually, he was my uncle, too, although I have a hard time dealing with that. I'm sure Brad has many good memories of their earlier times together, which will now haunt him. It seems we all have to go through this darn period of guilt as part of the grief process. I don't personally know anyone who was lucky enough to escape it."

"Nor do I," Dennis agreed.

"Oh, look," Emilia said as she pointed up and out toward the ocean. "There are about fifteen sea gulls out there in that one spot. There must be a school of fish right below them."

"You're right," Dennis said. "Look, there's a fishing boat headed that way."

"The sea is calm this morning," she said. "The sun is shining and all is right with the world." Emilia and Dennis ran along the shoreline until she was out of breath and had to stop and sit on one of the rock barriers that cut across the beach. They sat there until Emilia caught her breath and then they walked toward the steps leading up to the house.

"I wonder where Brad is?" Emilia asked. "He said he was coming out on the deck after Paul left."

"I guess he changed his mind." Dennis said. "We'll find him somewhere in the house. I think we should take Brad out to lunch. How's that sound?"

"Sounds good to me," Emilia said. "Come on, I'll race you to the steps."

Jeff was watching from the kitchen window as Emilia and Dennis ran across the beach to the steps. How happy they look he thought. He almost felt bad about what he had to do, but it was inevitable.

He turned from the window when he heard Brad moan. Jeff could see Brad was coming to, so he quickly took out his handkerchief and used it as a gag so that Brad would not be able to call out. Jeff wondered how long he would have to wait for them to come to the kitchen to look for Brad.

Jeff heard them open the sliding doors into the dining room. Just then, he heard the phone ring and they both went into the living room.

Emilia sat down on the sofa as Dennis answered the phone. She could tell by the look on his face that it was not good news. She guessed by the gist of the conversation that he was either talking to Chief Archer or Agent Lawson. After Dennis hung up, he came over and sat down on the sofa with her.

"What's wrong?" Emilia asked.

"I'm afraid I've got some bad news," Dennis said. "We're not out of the woods yet. They are almost certain Jeff Owensford was not on the boat when it exploded." Emilia felt a sensation of pins and needles that started in her feet and slowly traveled to the top of her head. She had heard people say that their skin crawled and she never understood what they meant until now.

"Who was on the phone?" she asked.

"It was Chief Archer," Dennis replied. "He wanted to warn me to be on guard. He thinks Jeff Owensford might try to come here to the house."

"How do they know he wasn't on the boat?" Emilia asked.

"Agent Lawson had some of his men circulate a picture of Jeff Owensford around the area," Dennis said. "The owner of a small bar at the end of the dock said he remembered the man sitting at a small table next to the window when all the commotion was going on. He said most of his customers ran outside to see what happened, but that this individual just watched from the window. He doesn't remember him ever being in his establishment before. The man stayed until the bar closed."

"What do we do now?" Emilia asked with a quiver in her voice. She was so happy just minutes before and now her insides were shaking. She was sitting with her legs crossed and she leaned forward and wrapped her arms tightly around her legs. Dennis reached over and pulled her back and held her in his arms.

"The first thing you're going to do is relax," he said. "Everything will be all right. They're looking for him now. I'm going outside and talk to the men Agent Lawson has watching the house. I'll be right back. You find Brad and tell him what's happened." Emilia tried to calm down as Dennis suggested. She knew he felt the physical tightness in her loosen as she concentrated and tried to relax. She sensed a loving tenderness as he held her a few minutes more before he reluctantly stood up to go. He bent over to give her a kiss and said he'd be right back. She heard the front door open and close. Emilia wondered where Brad was. She thought it strange he didn't hear the phone ring and come to the living room to find out who called.

Jeff and Brad both heard the phone ring. Jeff listened at the kitchen door while Brad sat helpless, tied and gagged on a kitchen chair. Jeff could hear most of the conversation when Dennis McClelland was talking on the phone, but then as Emilia and Dennis talked, he couldn't quite make out what they were saying. Then he heard the front door open and close and he wasn't sure who left. Things were not going quite the way he planned.

As Dennis closed the front door, he looked around and noticed Agent Lawson's men sitting in their car a few yards down the driveway. He walked over to ask if they heard about Jeff Owensford. They said they were notified and assured Dennis that their surveillance revealed nothing out of the ordinary.

Dennis decided he wanted to check for himself, at least the area in close proximity to the house. He walked around the right side of the house to the back deck, where he stopped and looked up and down the beach. The entire beach, as far as the eye could see, was as uninhabited as it was when he and Emilia were down there a short time ago. Dennis then walked across the back deck and started around the left side of the house. He was almost to the front of the house when he happened to glance toward the row of large pine trees that bordered the edge of Brad's property on this side of the house. He saw something behind the trees, but he wasn't sure what it was.

As Dennis walked in the direction of the trees and drew nearer to them, he was able to make out the silhouette of a car parked behind the trees. He stopped in his tracks when he realized he should get Agent Lawson's men for backup. Dennis knew it would be foolish to investigate on his own because he had no way of knowing whether there was anyone in the car.

Dennis ran around to the front of the house and motioned for Agent Lawson's men. They immediately got out of the car and ran to Dennis, who silently pointed to what he saw through the trees. As the three of them neared the line of trees, they separated and each approached the car from a different direction with their guns drawn.

They approached with caution until they were close enough to determine that the car was empty. When they looked in the glove compartment, the papers there indicated it was a rental car. Dennis walked back to their car with them and waited while they called it in. They told him they should have the rental information within minutes. Dennis sensed something was wrong. As soon as the information on the car came through, he decided he would return to the house to keep an eye on Emilia.

When Dennis left the house, Emilia went half way up the steps and called Brad's name. When he didn't answer, she started back down the steps. She couldn't imagine where he was. Perhaps his housekeeper would know she thought and headed for the kitchen.

Jeff heard Emilia call Brad's name and run up the steps. Then he listened as she came back down. He knew she would be coming to the kitchen any minute. He looked over at Brad and could see the fear and anxiety in his eyes. Jeff stood behind the kitchen door as it swung open.

Emilia started into the kitchen and immediately saw Brad on the chair with blood on the side of his face. She ran toward him as Jeff closed the door, blocking her exit, and began to laugh. Emilia's feet were frozen to the spot where she stood. She was unable to turn around. She looked into Brad's terror stricken eyes and thought she was going to faint. She grabbed the edge of the table and forced herself to turn and face Jeff Owensford. She heard herself gasp when she noticed the dried blood on his shirt and pants. She saw a face ugly and contorted with hate.

"Why are you doing this?" Emilia cried out. "What has Brad ever done to you?" As frightened as she was, Emilia stepped in front of Brad to protect him. "He's your brother."

"Not really," Jeff whispered. "He's only my half-brother." As soon as Jeff said the words, Emilia noticed an immediate change in his demeanor. Jeff's facial expression, which moments before was contorted with rage, slowly turned to one of amazement. "I remember now," he said.

As Emilia wondered what it was he remembered, Jeff suddenly broke down and sobbed as though his heart would break. Emilia turned around and looked down at Brad to see if his eyes showed any indication of knowing what Jeff was talking about. Although Jeff had a gun, Emilia realized he seemed to have forgotten they were even there. She quickly pulled down the gag that was in Brad's mouth.

"Jeff," Brad said. "What are you talking about? What do you mean half-brother?"

Emilia watched as Jeff struggled to control himself. "I mean that you are my half-brother," Jeff said. "That's why I hated you all these years, but I must have blocked it out because I didn't want to face it." Emilia could see that Jeff appeared to be more rational as he spoke in a quiet voice. She assumed that this was probably the behavior pattern the doctor had seen.

"But I still don't understand," Brad said. "We look enough alike to be twins."

"Then we must both look like our mother," Jeff said. "Because we didn't have the same father."

"Where did you ever get that idea?" Brad asked. "I've never heard anyone say anything that would even suggest such a thing."

"Because I overheard them," Jeff said. "Our mother was raped. I heard father tell the priest about it. He told him that he made up his mind, and promised mother as well, that he would love the child as his own. That child must have been me. But father didn't love me as his own. He always favored you. I knew why and I despised you. That's when I decided to be everything you were not. When father found out I was working for the APLA, he used that as an excuse to disinherit me. But I knew it was really because I was not his biological son as you were." Emilia looked from one to the other as she wondered where Dennis was.

"Why are you so sure the child was you and not me?" Brad asked. Emilia waited for Jeff's reaction to a possibility she felt sure never occurred to him before. Jeff thought about what Brad said for several minutes before he replied.

"Because I was the one who never fit in," Jeff said. "I was the maverick who preferred to be alone, who was devoid of a normal conscience, who couldn't interact socially, who believed everyone plotted against him, and who even heard voices tell him what to do. I sensed there was something wrong with me, although I never admitted it. I knew I was different. I remember father told the priest that the man who raped mother was mentally unbalanced and I figured I inherited the strange feelings that plagued me from him. That was the obvious explanation I came up with."

"But you were wrong," Brad said. "The child you heard them talk about was me. Father told me himself before he died. There was a reason he appeared to favor me. It was because he bent over backwards to make sure he treated me the same as you so that mother would never have cause to doubt that he loved me as his own. He worked so hard at proving this that he appeared to favor me. But it wasn't true. I'm sure he loved you as much, if not more, than me. If I had known what you were thinking all these years, I would have told you. I never did because I wanted to spare you. You've hated me all these years and for nothing. What a waste for us both." Emilia sensed that Jeff realized Brad was telling him the truth. She watched him struggle with this new revelation and wondered how he was going to react.

Jeff realized the bitterness, hatred and jealousy that gnawed at him over the years and was now about to destroy him was based on a lie. The horrendous truth was that he fabricated the lie himself and was now about to face the consequences. Jeff also knew that Brad, even though he knew the truth, never used it in any way to undermine or hurt him. Emilia could see in Jeff's eyes that he accepted what Brad told him.

"Can I untie Brad?" Emilia asked. "Please don't hurt him." She watched as Jeff put the gun back in his pocket and walked over to them.

"I'll do it," Jeff said. "Brad, I don't know what to say. I did some terrible things over the years. I can't change that now. It's too late." He untied Brad's hands. Brad grabbed Jeff's arm as he turned to walk away.

"Jeff, please don't run," Brad said. "I'll help you. If you do have a mental problem, Dr. Scott told Joyce they have medication for it. I know they can help you."

"I'm afraid it's too late," Jeff said. "They're probably looking for me right now. I could never stand to be locked up. I'm sorry, but I've got to go. You'll never see me again." Emilia felt the tears sting her eyes as Jeff threw his arms around Brad and they embraced. Then Jeff ran from the room.

- *TWENTY-NINE* -

Dennis was just coming into the house as Jeff ran from the kitchen. Jeff pushed him aside, knocking him to the floor, as he ran into the dining room and out the sliding glass doors onto the deck.

Dennis struggled to his feet, then ran into the kitchen in time to see Emilia hold a wet towel to Brad's head.

"Thank God, you're all right," Dennis said with relief. "What happened to Brad?"

"I'll be OK," Brad said. "Did you see Jeff?"

"See him?" Dennis asked. "He knocked me for a loop as I was coming into the house. I think he ran out the back. He's got a car parked behind the pine trees. I'll get Agent Lawson's men. Maybe we can catch him before he gets away."

"Be careful," Emilia said. "He's desperate."

"I will," Dennis shouted back as he ran to the front door.

By the time Dennis got back outside, he saw that Agent Lawson's men had already heard the car start and they turned in time to see Jeff Owensford pull out. He was driving erratically and almost hit their car as he sped down the drive. The agents slowed up long enough for Dennis to jump into the back seat. As they followed the car with their siren on, the agent seated on the passenger side of the front seat used the radio to alert the local police.

Jeff Owensford heard the siren and looked into his rear view mirror. He knew the police would have a roadblock set up in Sandwich and he'd never be able to drive over the bridge to get off the Cape. He turned in the opposite direction toward Sandy Neck. The FBI was gaining and almost directly behind him as he approached the

Sandwich Railroad tracks that crossed over 6A in Sandy Neck.

Jeff saw the light flashing and floored the gas pedal. He barely made it over the tracks when the train went by. He looked in the rear view mirror and saw that the other car was unable to stop and swerved into a cranberry bog. Jeff turned off Route 6A onto Rte. 138 and headed for Hyannis Airport. The APLA had its own hanger there and he hoped the airplane was not in use and a pilot was available.

As Jeff sped down the highway, Dennis picked himself up off the floor in the back seat of the car. He noticed that the FBI agents appeared dazed and realized they had probably smacked their heads when the car came to such an abrupt stop. Dennis got out of the car and opened the front door of the passenger's side and helped the one man out. By this time, others had come running to help and got the other one out. Dennis and the agents waited to be picked up by the local police.

Dennis saw that it was Chief Archer himself who came to get them. Dennis got in the front seat with Chief Archer and the two FBI men got in the back.

"Which way was he headed?" Chief Archer asked.

"Toward Sandy Neck," Dennis said. "At least he was the last time we saw him."

"He might be heading for the airport," Chief Archer said. "We'll put out an APB and I'll alert the airport police to be on the lookout for anyone fitting his description with a Chicago destination. In the meantime, we'll search around the area where he was last seen."

Jeff traveled at the speed limit so he wouldn't draw any attention to himself. He felt certain he'd be all right if he could just make it to the airport without being stopped. Once again my luck has held out he thought as he turned into the airport. He drove directly to the hanger where the APLA housed its own plane. His heart was pounding as he walked to the hanger and looked inside. He couldn't believe his eyes. The plane was there and the pilot was getting ready to leave.

Jeff ran up to the pilot, showed him his identification and told him he needed to go to Chicago at once. The pilot said he did not recognize the name and would have to get an OK from the CEO. Jeff gave him a number to call for authorization. It was only a few minutes before the pilot returned and said they could take off at once.

As the plane taxied out onto the runway to await instructions for takeoff, Jeff saw a police car pull up at the main gate of the airport. He watched as two policemen got out and hurried into the airport. He asked the pilot if there was anyone in the airport who knew he had a passenger. After the pilot assured him there was no one, Jeff was able to lean back and relax. As the plane taxied down the runway, Jeff knew he didn't need to worry about being picked up in Chicago since they wouldn't be looking for him to arrive on a private plane. But he realized they were probably watching his apartment. He would have to find somewhere else to stay he thought. But he didn't need to worry about it now. He closed his eyes and listened to the steady hum of the motor as he drifted off to sleep.

Dennis went with Chief Archer when he dropped off the two FBI men in Sandwich after they searched the area for about an hour and came up with nothing. Dennis and Chief Archer then headed back to Brad's house. When they got there, Dennis looked for Emilia and found her and Brad sitting on the sofa in the living room. He saw that Brad was holding an ice pack on his head.

"You look a little better," Dennis said. "You have a little more color in your face than when I left."

"Did you catch Jeff?" Emilia asked.

"No, we didn't," Dennis said. "We almost had him but he got away."

"I put out an APB on him," Chief Archer said. "He'll be caught, it's just a matter of time."

"I imagine he'll try to get back to Chicago," Emilia said. "He knows influential people there who could help him leave the country."

"I'm sure the FBI is aware of that," Dennis said. "He won't have much time to make arrangements. The longer it takes him, the less chance he'll have to get away. Even the APLA will have its hands full with this one."

"I'm not sure they'll go out on a limb for him," Chief Archer said. "As long as they feel confident that there's no physical evidence to connect Jeff Owensford to their organization, they will more than likely play innocent."

"That would be consistent with their despicable reputation," Emilia said. "I hope the FBI is able to prove the connection, with full media coverage, and make it stick in court. That, along with the loss of Brad's money, should be enough to put them out of business."

"I hope it turns out that way," Brad said. "Chief, how about staying for lunch?" Emilia gave Brad a hand up as he took off the ice pack and walked to the door. "I don't know what happened to my housekeeper. I haven't seen her since all this confusion started."

"I'll see if she's in the kitchen," Emilia said as she followed Brad to the door.

Dennis and Chief Archer remained in the living room while Emilia and Brad went to find the housekeeper. Dennis got up and walked to the window to look out at the ocean. His thoughts turned to Emilia and how happy they were just a few hours ago. He wished this whole dilemma would soon be cleared up. He'd almost forgotten what it was like to have a normal routine day. His thoughts were interrupted as Emilia came back into the room.

"Denny, we can't find her anywhere," she said. "Brad is quite concerned."

"Did you check the whole house?" Chief Archer asked.

"We checked everywhere but the basement," Emilia said. "Maybe I better look down there."

"No," Dennis said. "I'll go down and check it out."

"I'll go with you," Chief Archer said. They went out to the hall and Emilia waited as Dennis unlocked the door and he and Chief Archer went down the steps. She was still standing at the top of the steps when Chief Archer ran back up and said he had to call an ambulance. Emilia ran down the steps to see what happened.

She looked in the laundry room and saw Dennis kneeling beside Brad's housekeeper. Emilia felt faint and almost gagged at the sight of the blood splattered on the side of the washer and dryer. She pulled herself together and walked over to kneel down beside Dennis.

"Is she still alive?" Emilia whispered. "She doesn't look like she's breathing."

"She's in bad shape," Dennis said. "We could barely detect a pulse. Maybe you better go back upstairs and tell Brad. But don't let him come down. There's nothing he can do. He's been through enough today."

Emilia passed Chief Archer on her way back up the steps. Brad was already at the top of the steps wondering what was going on. Emilia took him by the arm and walked him into the living room. She then told him what they found downstairs in the basement. He wanted to go down but she held onto his arm and told him Dennis said there was nothing he could do. The ambulance was on the way.

"Do you think she'll make it?" Brad asked. "I feel so bad. She was just an innocent bystander. She certainly didn't deserve that."

"No, she didn't," Emilia agreed. Then she sensed that Brad suddenly realized what she thought of at once, that Jeff would be charged with murder if she didn't pull through. Just then, Emilia heard a siren and knew it was the ambulance coming up the driveway. She opened the door and showed them where to go. They did as much as they could before they left for the hospital.

Emilia and Dennis went out on the back deck and left Brad and Chief Archer in the living room. They walked over to the railing and looked out at the ocean.

"This has been quite a day," Emilia said. "I wonder where Jeff Owensford is now. I know he's done some terrible things over the years and there is no excuse. But when I think of the tortured life he led, self-inflicted by his misunderstanding of a conversation he overheard when a child, I could just cry. What a waste."

"I don't understand what you mean," Dennis said. Emilia forgot Dennis didn't know what went on in the kitchen before Jeff ran out, so she told him the whole thing. After she was through, he shook his head in disbelief. "That explains a lot. It's too bad that it lay festering in Jeff's subconscious all those years. Well, I hope he's more at peace, wherever he is."

At that very moment, Jeff Owensford was stepping off the plane in Chicago. When the pilot landed, he taxied off the main runway and over to the APLA hanger. Jeff didn't even have to walk through the main terminal to get out.

When the cab picked him up, Jeff told the driver to take him into town. He still didn't know exactly where to go. Then he decided on Paul's house. He didn't think the FBI would have his house staked out. He wondered if Paul was home yet. He might not have been able to get a flight right away he thought. Well, he knew he had no other choice, so he gave the cab driver Paul's street address.

Jeff looked around when the cab pulled up and didn't notice anything unusual. He paid the driver and walked up to Paul's door as the cab pulled away. Jeff rang the doorbell and Paul opened the door. Jeff could see the fear written all over Paul's face when he saw who stood outside his door. He saw the initial flush turn to an ashen color in just seconds.

"Can I come in?" Jeff asked. He didn't wait for an answer, just brushed past Paul and into the living room. Jeff could see that Paul was hesitant about closing the door. "You can close the door. I'm not here to hurt you."

"What do you want then?" Paul asked as he closed the door. "I don't want any part of you."

"I know that," Jeff said. "I know there's no excuse for what I did to you years ago. But there is one last thing I want you to do for me."

"You must really be crazy?" Paul shouted. "I wouldn't do a thing for you. I just want you to get out and leave me alone." Jeff could see that Paul was trembling and he suddenly felt sorry for him. This was a new experience for Jeff and he didn't know how to handle it. He watched Paul's expression change when he took a good look and noticed the difference in him. It was then that Paul calmed down a little.

"It's not for me," Jeff said. "It's for Brad."

"You want me to do something for Brad?" Paul asked. Jeff sensed that Paul was completely bewildered by the change in him and viewed it with some suspicion. He realized he'd probably have to share with Paul what he found out in order to obtain his help. I owe him that much anyway he thought. Jeff told Paul exactly what went on in Brad's kitchen this morning and ended up by apologizing for the suffering he caused Paul as well.

"I don't know what to say," Paul said.

"Don't say anything," Jeff said. "Just say you'll help me." Jeff waited as Paul considered. "Please, we don't have much time."

"What do you want me to do?" Paul asked.

"I want you to go with me to my bank," Jeff said. "I'm going to give you some papers I have in a safety deposit box there. I want you to make sure Brad gets them. Maybe Dennis McClelland could come for them."

"What are they?" Paul asked.

"They will prove my connection with the APLA," Jeff said. "There's also a complete agenda of their past, present and projected future activities. When this agenda is made public, it will be enough to put them out of business. Perhaps it will make up for some of the terrible things I've done." Jeff suddenly felt the beginning of a migraine headache and he felt nauseous as his stomach churned. He sat down on the nearest chair and leaned forward with his head in his hands.

"Are you all right?" Paul asked.

"It's one of my headaches," Jeff said. "I'll take a pill as soon as we get those papers from the bank. You know the FBI is looking for me, don't you?"

"Yes, I know," Paul said.

"I'll leave you as soon as I hand you the papers," Jeff said. "I know I can trust you."

"Where will you go?" Paul asked.

"I don't know," Jeff said. "I'm just going away."

Emilia, Dennis and Brad went out to lunch after Chief Archer left. Then they stopped at the hospital and heard the good news that the doctor expected Brad's housekeeper to make a full recovery.

When they returned home and opened the door, the ringing of the phone cut through the stillness of the house. Brad ran into the living room to answer. As Emilia walked into the room, she was surprised when Brad said Paul Freedman wanted to talk to her. After she took the phone, Brad got them some iced tea and he and Dennis sat down.

"Hi, Paul," she said. "What's up?"

"I just left Jeff. He gave me some papers for Brad that will prove Jeff's connection to the APLA. There's also an agenda of their past, present and projected future activities. Jeff said when it's made public, it should be enough to vindicate Brad of any connection to them and put them out of business for good. Jeff hoped this might make up in part for some of the terrible things he did over the years."

"How did Jeff manage to get there?" Emilia asked.

"I don't know," Paul said. "He told me what he found out this morning about his mother and father."

"How is he?" she asked.

"He's still having a problem with the headaches," Paul said. "But he's like a different person. He said we would never see him again."

"He told us that also," Emilia said. "Do you want Dennis to fly out there and pick up the papers?"

"I think that might be best," Paul said. "I sure wouldn't want them to fall into the wrong hands. Let me know when he's coming and I'll meet him at the airport."

"I'll do that," Emilia said. "Take care."

After she hung up, she told Brad and Dennis everything that Paul said.

"I wonder if Jeff will get away?" Brad asked.

"I don't know," Emilia said. She went and sat down on the sofa next to Dennis and took a sip of her tea. "If he does, I wonder where he'll end up or if we'll ever see him again." Emilia knew this was not something she would wonder about too long as Dennis put his arm around her and drew her close.

About the Author

After working for over twenty years in a corporate environment, Carol Roth decided to follow the advice of friends and try her hand at writing fiction. *Forget Me Not* is the result of that endeavor.

Carol resides in Allegheny County, Pennsylvania with her husband.